# In Too Deep

## Patricia H. Rushford

D0950448

# Jennie McGrady Mystery Series

9608

# In Too Deep

## Patricia H. Rushford

**BETHANY HOUSE PUBLISHERS**
MINNEAPOLIS, MINNESOTA 55438

*In Too Deep*
Copyright © 1996
Patricia Rushford

Cover illustration by Andrea Jorgenson

Published by Bethany House Publishers
A Ministry of Bethany Fellowship, Inc.
11300 Hampshire Avenue South
Minneapolis, Minnesota 55438

Printed in the United States of America.

---

**Library of Congress Cataloging-in-Publication Data**

Rushford, Patricia H.
  In Too Deep / Patricia H. Rushford.
      p.  cm. — (The Jennie McGrady mystery series ; 8)
  Summary: Jennie becomes involved when someone breaks into the high school to steal chemicals and then the chemistry teacher is found shot dead.
  ISBN 1–55661–561–2 (pbk.)
  [1.  Mystery and detective stories.  2.  Christian life—Fiction.  I. Title.  II. Series.  III. Series: Rushford, Patricia H. Jennie McGrady mystery series ; 8.
PZ7.R8962In    1996
[Fic]—dc20                                          96–25285
                                                         CIP
                                                          AC

---

To Mrs. Rockne's fourth-grade class
at Grand Forks Christian School

A special thank you to the Vancouver and Camas
Police Departments in Washington State—especially
to Officer Jane McNicholas and Officer Paul Pierce
for lending valuable insight and authenticity.

PATRICIA RUSHFORD is an award-winning writer, speaker, and teacher who has published numerous articles and more than twenty books, including *What Kids Need Most in a Mom, The Jack and Jill Syndrome: Healing for Broken Children*, and her first young adult novel, *Kristen's Choice*. She is a registered nurse and has a master's degree in counseling from Western Evangelical Seminary. She and her husband, Ron, live in Washington State and have two grown children, six grandchildren, and lots of nephews and nieces.

Pat has been reading mysteries for as long as she can remember and is delighted to be writing a series of her own. She is a member of Mystery Writers of America, Sisters in Crime, Society of Children's Book Writers and Illustrators, and several other writing organizations. She is also co-director of Writer's Weekend at the Beach.

# 1

"You're going to work on the case, aren't you?" Lisa Calhoun's green eyes sparkled with excitement as she followed Jennie into her bedroom and closed the door. "Come on, admit it."

Jennie McGrady shook her head. "No way." The *case* her cousin was talking about involved a burglary at Trinity High. Someone had broken into the chemistry lab and stolen chemicals and supplies. The police suspected whoever did it planned to set up a meth lab. "I'm going to talk to Mr. Mancini about my chemistry project. I told you that." Jennie yanked off her T-shirt and ducked into her closet to get a short-sleeved white cotton shirt. She loved wearing white in the summer—especially when she had a tan.

"I know, but I can't believe the chem project is the only reason you're going. School doesn't start for three weeks."

"I'm home-schooled, remember?" Being a single parent, Jennie's mom had created a part home-school, part private school situation so Jennie could be home afternoons to baby-sit her five-year-old brother, Nick. "Besides, I want to get a head start. I told you that too."

Though Jennie rarely missed an opportunity to solve a crime, she had no intention of trying to track down the thief—especially not after what her friend with the Portland police had told her. Rocky (a.k.a. Dean Rockwell) had lectured her for an hour about the toxic chemicals involved in the making of clandestine drug labs. He'd called them "kitchens of death." *"These labs are deathtraps, Jennie,"* he'd said. *"You don't want to have anything to do with this case."* With a pained look in his blue eyes and a catch in his voice he'd told her about a friend of his who'd accidentally triggered a booby trap in a meth lab. Just breathing in the chemical fumes for a few seconds had caused the officer's lungs to collapse. Rocky had other stories too—all of them tragic—and convincing.

Jennie pushed the disturbing thoughts aside. "Anyway," she continued, "it's too dangerous."

"That hasn't stopped you before." Lisa joined her in the small walk-in closet and wrinkled her nose. "We really need to take you shopping. You have absolutely nothing to wear for school this year."

Jennie pulled the white shirt off the hanger and slipped it on. Glancing around her closet, she had to agree. She and her mom had cleaned out everything she'd either worn to death or that no longer fit—which was just about everything she owned. "Maybe later." She tucked the shirttail into her faded jeans, kicked off her sneakers, and stuffed her feet into a pair of leather loafers. "Where'd I put my vest?"

"It's on the bed." Lisa retrieved the denim vest and held it while Jennie slipped her arms into it.

Jennie moved to her dresser, brushed her long dark hair, and pulled it into a ponytail. She picked up a small gold necklace, secured it around her neck, and opened the heart that dangled from the chain.

"What's that?"

"A locket—Hannah sent it to me. Says I should wear it all the time so I'll never forget her. Like that could happen." Hannah, Jennie's four-year-old neighbor girl and victim of a kidnapping, had stayed with them as a foster child for a couple of weeks before going to live with her grandparents in Arizona. Jennie had rescued the girl and wanted very much to make her part of the McGrady family, but it didn't happen.

"You still miss her, don't you?"

"Yeah." Jennie sighed, then glanced down at the adorable flaxen-haired child in the small photo. "But she seems happy—I guess that's what really matters. Her grandparents are nice—they wrote a letter to us saying how much they appreciated our taking care of her."

"I thought you were going to Arizona to visit them."

"I wanted to, but when have I had a chance?"

Lisa chuckled. "I guess you have been pretty busy. Maybe you still can before school starts."

"Maybe. Mom and I talked about my going down in a couple of months—maybe over Labor Day weekend." Jennie closed the locket, then let it drop against her chest. "But that's a ways off. Are you coming with me to the school?"

Lisa tipped her head to one side as her gaze met Jennie's. "Well, if you were going to investigate the theft, I might, but if you're really only going to talk about chemistry, I'll pass."

"What, and miss the chance to hear about the molecular structure of acetylsalicylic acid?"

"Yeah—like that really excites me. Honestly, Jen, sometimes I think you're weird."

Jennie chuckled. "Different strokes." Actually, Jennie wasn't all that excited about chemistry. She mainly wanted a high grade-point average for college, where she planned to study law.

"I know. I know. It isn't that I hate chemistry—not really," Lisa said as she headed for the door, her copper-colored curls swaying as she walked. "It's just that I don't think Mr. Mancini likes me, and the feeling is mutual."

"Why?"

"Let's just say he doesn't have much patience for students with less than a four-point average." Without turning around Lisa added, "Allison and B.J. invited us to go swimming.

Why don't you meet me there after you talk to Mr. Mancini?"

"Sounds great as long as Mom doesn't need me to baby-sit Nick."

"She doesn't. I already asked."

After Lisa left, Jennie grabbed her leather backpack and followed the giggling sounds to the kitchen to say goodbye to her mom and brother. Five-year-old Nick greeted her with a chocolate grin. "Mom's makin' brownies and she's lettin' me lick the bowl."

"Can I have some?"

"Nope."

"Nick." The warning in Susan McGrady's voice changed his mind.

"Okay. Long as you don't be a pig." Nick released his hold on the glass bowl and slid it toward his sister.

"Do I look like a pig?" Jennie snuffled and snorted and blew a raspberry against the side of his neck. Nick wiggled and squealed, arms and legs flying.

"Whoa." She caught him just as he slipped off the tall wicker stool. The spatula slapped a wide streak of chocolate across her cheek.

"Jennie, quit teasing him. You'll end up with brownie mix all over yourself." Mom grabbed a washcloth from a drawer, wet it, and tossed it to Jennie. "You'd better hustle or you'll be late for your appointment."

"I'm going." She washed her face, then scooped up a mass of the silky chocolate mixture with her finger and stuck it in her mouth. When she'd licked her finger clean, she washed her hands in the sink and grabbed her keys from the hook by the kitchen door. "Do you mind if I go over to the Beaumonts' to swim this afternoon?"

"Not a problem as long as you're home by five. Michael's coming over for dinner. We have something we'd like to talk to you about."

"Sure." Jennie's good mood faded as she rummaged

through a clean laundry basket for her swimsuit and a towel. She stuffed them in a canvas beach bag, kissed Mom and Nick goodbye, and left.

"Jennie! Wait!" Nick caught up to her on the porch. "I gotta ax you somethin'."

"Can't it wait till tonight? I have to go."

His bony little shoulders rose and fell in an exaggerated sigh. "I guess so."

"Okay," Jennie lowered herself onto the top step. "I suppose I can spare a couple of minutes."

Nick hunkered down with his elbows resting on his knees. "If Mommy marries Michael and my real daddy comes back, will I have two daddies?"

The question took Jennie by surprise. Nick rarely talked about Dad since Mom brought Michael home. "Not exactly." Jennie pulled Nick onto her lap and hugged him. "Michael would be your stepdad."

"Oh . . . but what if my real dad comes home and finds out that Michael is my other dad? Won't he be sad?"

"Um—I don't think Dad will come back. But I know he'd want you to have a stepdad like Michael. Anyway, I thought you loved Michael?"

"I do—him and me is buddies."

"How come you're asking all these questions about Dad?"

"'Cause you and Mama never show me his pictures anymore, and I think that would make him sad."

Before Michael came along, she, Nick, and Mom would go through the photo album and talk about Dad's coming back someday. Then Mom decided to get on with her life. End of story. "Tell you what. I miss seeing Dad's pictures too. Maybe tonight we can look at them before you go to bed. But right now, I gotta go."

Nick wrapped his wiry arms around her neck, gave her

one of his super-duper bear hugs, and deposited a chocolate kiss on her mouth.

By the time she reached her Mustang, Jennie felt downright depressed. There were no clouds in the late summer sky; they were all in her head.

It didn't take a genius to figure out what Mom and her fiancé wanted to discuss. They had been engaged on and off for several months, and Jennie suspected tonight's dinner plans included setting a wedding date. At first, Jennie had been furious that her mom would even think of getting married. Now she didn't know what to think.

"Come off it, McGrady," Jennie muttered to herself as she twisted the key in the ignition. "Michael's a great guy."

*But he's not Dad.* Jennie frowned and tried to put the entire mess out of her mind. Her parents had made their decisions, and there wasn't much she could do about it. Or was there? Maybe if she told Mom that Dad was still alive it would make a difference. *Don't even think it, McGrady. You promised Dad and the government you would keep his secret.*

"It just isn't fair," she said aloud.

*"Life isn't fair,"* her father had responded when she'd said those same words to him.

"Oh, Dad," Jennie murmured, "please come home. Sometimes I wish I hadn't tried to find you. In some ways it was better not knowing."

Dad worked for the DEA, the Drug Enforcement Agency, as an undercover agent and supposedly died five years ago in a plane crash. Besides Jennie, only a few key government officials knew he was still alive. Coming home would pose a danger to him and his family. He'd changed his identity several times. Still, Jennie had this dream that he and Mom would someday get back together. Fat chance of that happening now.

Jennie pulled to a stop at a red light, wishing she could control her emotions as easily as she could her car. Even if

Mom knew Dad was alive, she probably wouldn't change her mind. Her parents were officially divorced—Mom had done that after meeting Michael so she wouldn't have to wait the full seven years it took to have someone declared legally dead.

As Jennie approached Trinity Center, she took a deep breath and shoved her memories and her feelings into the bottom drawer of her mind. The sun glinted off the blue metal roof, giving the multilevel complex the appearance of a peacock's tail. The building housed a private school as well as a church and day-care center. The church sat in the center with the school fanning out on either side—the grade school on one side and the high school on the other. Jennie drove down the steep, winding drive to the far parking lot, pulled into a space near the school office, and jogged inside.

"Hi, Jennie. What brings you here?" Mrs. Talbot's round face dimpled when she smiled. "I don't have your schedule done yet."

"I know. I'm here to see Mr. Mancini." Jennie adjusted the strap of her leather backpack, shifting it more securely over her left shoulder.

"Oh yes. You must be the student he was expecting. Said to send you on back." Mrs. Talbot turned her attention back to her computer and began typing.

"Thanks." Ignoring the butterflies that had mysteriously appeared in her stomach, Jennie hurried down the empty hall. Sunlight poured in through the windows that lined the hall on one side, turning the area into an oven. The air-conditioner did little to curb the powerful effect of solar heat.

The chemistry department was located at the end of the hallway. Jennie paused at the door and took a deep breath. An odd sensation crept up her spine—the kind you get when you know someone's watching you. She looked around, half expecting to see the secretary, or one of the other students.

The hall remained empty. Her only companion was her own elongated shadow on the wall.

Jennie shivered. *Stop it, McGrady. You're letting your imagination run wild again.* She was probably just nervous about meeting Mr. Mancini. The chemistry teacher was fairly new to Trinity. He'd come in during the last two weeks of school as a substitute for Dr. Adams, who'd had a stroke. Since Jennie had completed her studies early, she hadn't met him—which was fine with her. From what Lisa had said, he had the personality of a warthog.

Pushing the door to the chemistry lab open, Jennie stepped inside. The lights were out, giving the room the feel of an overcast day. Unlike most of the rooms, this one had only a bank of narrow windows near the roof. One of them had been left open. She paused to switch on the overhead fluorescent lights. "Mr. Mancini? It's me—Jennie McGrady."

The room felt cold next to the overheated hallway. She stepped farther into the room, letting the door close behind her. A pungent odor hung on the air. Cleaning solution maybe, and something else—like a match that had just been lit and blown out. The black counters glistened as though they'd recently been washed. Jennie set her bag on the floor and skimmed her hand across the shiny surface. Still damp.

A shuffling sound from the office at the back of the lab caught her attention. She hurried toward it and knocked. "Mr. Mancini?" she called again. When no one answered, Jennie tried the knob. The door opened easily, but the large, two-desk office was empty. Another door leading to a faculty parking lot stood ajar.

Jennie stepped outside to investigate. A steel gray car sat in a nearby parking space, but there was no sign of a teacher or anyone else. Whoever had been in the office was gone. The small sign on the building identified the space as Mancini's.

"This is too weird," Jennie said aloud. It was almost as if

someone had heard her come in and run away when she called. She doubted that person was Mancini. Unless she'd gotten the time wrong. Jennie glanced at her watch. One o'clock. That's when he'd said to meet him.

Jennie shrugged and stepped back into the office. Her curious gaze scanned the room. The smaller desk looked like it hadn't been used in a while. When school started it would be assigned to Mr. Mancini's lab assistant—usually a senior. The computer on Mr. Mancini's desk was on, and Jennie hit the space bar to eliminate the tropical fish screen saver. The screen was a jumble of figures and odd shapes—pentagons, hexagons, and circles. It looked like some sort of formula. She recognized a few of the symbols: NaOH—sodium hydroxide—and $Br_2$, which was bromine, and HCL or hydrochloric acid. It had been written by someone with a great deal more knowledge about chemistry than she had. Probably her teacher. She hoped it wasn't the makings of a pop quiz.

Mancini had to be around somewhere. An open briefcase sat near the computer. Papers were strewn all over the desk and some had fallen on the floor. Jennie stooped to pick them up and placed them on top of the pile. Maybe that had been the sound she'd heard. Papers falling.

Her teacher could have gone to the rest room or something. But through the back entrance? And why would he leave the door open?

The burglary. Jennie's heart lurched. Of course. What if the thief had come back? Maybe she'd interrupted him.

*Wait a minute. Calm down. Don't jump to conclusions.* She sank into the teacher's squeaky wooden chair and picked up the phone to call the police. An instant later she set it down. Maybe it wasn't a burglary. "It could have been the janitor," she said aloud, remembering the still-damp counters. "Everything looks spotless in the lab. And Mr. Olsen is hard of hearing."

Jennie took a deep breath and released it. *Okay*, she rationalized. *Mancini's car is in the parking lot, so he has to be around somewhere.* Best to find out before calling the police. Jennie retraced her steps through the lab and out the door. Halfway down the hall she remembered her backpack, thought about going back to retrieve it, and decided she could pick it up later.

"My, that was quick." Mrs. Talbot pushed away from her desk as Jennie approached.

"I haven't seen him yet."

"Oh?"

"Yeah. Kind of strange, really. I heard something in the office, but when I went to check, he wasn't there and the door to the faculty parking lot was open. His car is still there, but I got worried—I mean, he could have just gone out for a few minutes, but I got to thinking about the burglary and everything. Maybe we should call the police."

"Oh, dear, I hate to do that—in case it's a false alarm. Still, it does seem rather strange. When was your meeting?"

"At one." They both looked at the white-faced clock on the wall. It was now one-ten.

Mrs. Talbot frowned. "It's certainly not like Mr. Mancini to be late. He's the most punctual man I've ever met." She grabbed the phone and punched out a three-digit extension. "He isn't answering. Could be he had to step over to the church office for something." She punched out three more numbers. Into the phone she said, "Sarah—is Mr. Mancini over there?"

The church secretary's answer must have been no because Mrs. Talbot's frown lines deepened. "Um . . . we may have a problem. Could I speak with Pastor Dave or Michael?"

Mrs. Talbot focused a concerned gaze on Jennie and started to say something, then spoke into the phone instead. "Yes, Michael. Jennie's here to see Tom. His car is here, but he doesn't seem to be anywhere around. I wondered if you could check the rest room . . . he does have a heart condition, you know, and—yes. Thanks."

"He'll be right over." Miss Talbot hung up.

Jennie felt sick. She hadn't considered the possibility of a heart attack or injury. She hurried out to the hall and reached the men's rest room just as Michael did. He swung open the door and disappeared inside. Seconds later he emerged shaking his head. "He's not there."

Without waiting for a response he jogged past Jennie and Mrs. Talbot and headed for the chemistry department. Jennie raced after him.

"Don't come in," Michael yelled when Jennie pushed open the door a few seconds later.

"Is he hurt?" She glanced around, but saw no sign of Michael or Tom Mancini. "I can do CPR, Michael. If he's had a heart attack—"

"No!" Michael rose from between the two long counters, then came around to her join her. "That won't be necessary, Jennie." He placed an arm around her shoulders and guided her toward the door. "Mr. Mancini is dead."

# 2

"Dead?" Jennie tried to turn back. "But how do you—I mean, shouldn't we call 9–1–1? Shouldn't we do CPR?"

Michael tightened his hold on her shoulder and escorted her into the hall. "There's nothing either of us can do for him now."

After leading her back to the office and ordering her to stay put, he whispered something to Mrs. Talbot, ducked into the principal's office, and closed the door. She watched him through the open blinds as he picked up the phone. Michael sat on the edge of the desk and rubbed his forehead. Jennie strained to hear his side of the conversation, but the room didn't lend itself to eavesdropping—especially with Mrs. Talbot gasping and moaning in the background.

Michael glanced up and caught Jennie watching him and for a moment neither looked away. Michael was keeping something from her. She could read it in his stunned expression just before he broke eye contact and hung up. Running a hand through his wavy brown hair, he picked up the phone again. A few seconds later he opened the door. "All we can do now is wait." He looked at Jennie and sighed. "I think we'd better talk."

His look made Jennie feel guilty. Like she'd somehow been responsible. Maybe she had in a way. If she'd thought to look behind the counter, maybe . . . "D-did he have a heart attack?" She dropped into one of the chairs nearest the office door.

Michael folded his hands and closed his eyes as if saying a prayer. He looked up a moment later. "It's—there's no easy way to say this."

"Michael, what's going on?"

"It wasn't a heart attack. Mr. Mancini's been shot."

"Shot?" She couldn't have heard right. "Are you sure?"

Michael nodded. "I've called the police. They should be here any minute."

Jennie stared at the window behind him still trying to take it in. "But that means—" She couldn't quite finish the sentence. If Michael was right, Jennie may have been a breath away from witnessing a murder.

―――――――

Within minutes the entire complex had been invaded by swarms of police officers. At least a dozen official cars were parked at odd angles in front of the high school. They'd be securing the crime scene with their yellow tape, taking pictures of everything in the lab, dusting for fingerprints. And they'd be asking questions.

*Fingerprints.* Jennie's heart slammed into her throat and began beating so hard she could hardly breathe. Her fingerprints. Her backpack.

She wanted to run, even looked for an escape route. She hadn't done anything wrong, but the police might think otherwise. *Oh, come on, McGrady. Don't go jumping to conclusions. They're not going to think you did it.*

"Jennie?"

"Wha—" Her thoughts exploded as she caught sight of the blue uniform and the holstered gun.

Michael was standing beside a wiry young woman with short, dishwater blond hair. "This is Jennie McGrady—the student I was telling you about," he explained to the officer,

19

then turned to Jennie. "Jennie, this is Officer Phelps. She'd like to ask you a few questions. Are you okay with that?"

"Yeah." Jennie's voice sounded hollow, like she was in a tunnel. She stared at her folded hands, wondering how they got that way.

The officer continued to stand. She wrote something in her notebook, then said, "I understand you had a meeting with Mr. Mancini at one this afternoon."

Jennie swallowed hard. Her mouth felt dry. She wanted to look the officer in the eyes and say yes, but the word wouldn't come out and her eyes refused to travel up past the name badge. She could only nod in response. *What is wrong with you, McGrady?*

"Can you tell me what happened?"

She nodded again. "Um—would you mind if I got a drink of water first?"

Officer Phelps scrutinized Jennie and, after a few torturous seconds, said, "Sure. Go ahead."

Jennie stood up on legs about as sturdy as a block of Jell-O and made her way out of the office. After a short walk to the fountain and back, she felt almost normal. *Just tell them the truth, McGrady*, she reminded herself. *They're not going to blame you.*

"I'm sorry," she said as she returned to the office. "My mouth was so dry I could hardly talk." Jennie's gaze shifted from Officer Phelps to the young man standing next to her. The concerned look in his blue eyes melted her fears. "Rocky." She even managed a half-smile.

"You two know each other?" Phelps folded her arms across her chest, her dark brown gaze shifting from one to the other.

"Jennie and I go way back." Rocky rubbed his chin. "I heard she was here and thought I'd better check it out. Jennie has a habit of playing junior detective."

"I was about to question her," Phelps said. "Want to stick around?"

*Oh, please stay*, Jennie pleaded silently. *Please.* Somehow having Rocky there made her feel more at ease and in control.

"Sure. I've got a few questions of my own. Like what were you doing here? I thought I told you not to get involved in the burglary investigation."

Jennie shook her head. "I wasn't. Honest. After you told me about the meth labs, I decided to take your advice. I was just here to talk to Mr. Mancini about my chemistry project."

"I know you, Jennie. I know how your mind works."

Rocky didn't believe her. Jennie felt the panic rising again. Okay, so maybe she wasn't being entirely honest with him or herself. She hadn't intended to investigate the theft, but if the subject had come up she might have asked a few questions. "I came to the school to talk to Mr. Mancini about chemistry. Only, when I got here I couldn't find him." Jennie went on to tell them about the noise she'd heard, trying to retrace her steps and give them every detail she could remember.

"You were in the lab, but you didn't find the body?" Phelps paused in her note taking, suspicion evident in her serious features.

"N-no—I never dreamed he'd be dead. I just thought he'd forgotten our appointment or had to make a quick trip to the rest room or maybe he got held up talking to someone."

"Mrs. Talbot told us you were concerned about a second burglary."

"Yes. Um—I wasn't sure what to think with the back door standing open. I started to call you guys but decided I'd better talk to Mrs. Talbot first. That's why I went back to the office."

"Okay." Phelps flipped back through her notes, then asked for and wrote down Jennie's address and phone number. "I think that'll do it for now." She glanced up at Rocky. "I'm heading back over to the lab. You coming?"

"In a minute."

Phelps hesitated as though she wanted to say something, then turned abruptly and left. Rocky watched her go, then settled his gaze on Jennie. "You going to be okay?"

"I—I think so. I feel terrible about not finding Mr. Mancini's body when I was in the lab. If I'd gotten to him I might have been able to—"

"Don't. It's better you didn't see it. Of course, it is possible the shooting took place after you'd came back here to talk to Mrs. Talbot."

"I don't think so. There was this funny smell in the lab—disinfectant and something else—like sulfur. I didn't think much about it at the time, but it could have been from a gun being shot. I mean—I didn't hear a shot, but the killer could have used a silencer."

"I know I've said this before, Jennie, but you've got to stop getting involved in these criminal cases. You've been lucky so far, but sooner or later—"

"I wasn't getting involved. I told you—"

"Look," Rocky interrupted, "maybe you did go to see Mancini about schoolwork, or maybe you went to question him about the theft. It doesn't really matter. The thing is, you could have been killed in there. And from what you've told us, the danger isn't over. If the guy was still in the office when you walked in, and if you announced your arrival like you said, he knows who you are."

"But I didn't see anything."

"Maybe not, but he doesn't know that."

"Can I go now?"

"Not yet. Lieutenant Rastovski will probably want to talk to you after he finishes up in the lab."

"Well, can I at least get my book bag? I left it in the lab."

"That was yours?" He shook his head. "I don't think

you'll be seeing it for a while. It'll be processed as part of the evidence."

"Oh no. You can't—it's got my notebook and my keys—and my driver's license."

"Sorry, Jennie, you know the routine. I'm sure someone around here can give you a ride home."

"Am I a suspect?"

"Everyone is. You, Michael, even Mrs. Talbot."

"That's ridiculous."

Rocky shifted from one foot to the other. "A man's been found dead. We have to pursue every possible lead."

"I know. It's just that—"

The radio hooked to his collar made a scratchy sound and he ducked his head to talk into it. "David 4—on my way." More static.

Jennie wondered how they ever managed to understand each other.

"Ten-four." Rocky spoke into his lapel mike again, then squeezed her shoulder. "I gotta get back to work. You hang in there. Um—if you need to talk about what happened—well, just let me know."

"Sure."

After promising to call her later, Rocky mumbled something unintelligible and left.

She was alone in the office now. Both Mrs. Talbot and Michael had disappeared. Probably being questioned some more. At the far end of the hall, several police officers milled around outside the lab. She thought about heading down that way to ask a few questions of her own but decided it wouldn't do any good.

Unable to sit still, Jennie paced from the office door to the main entrance, then wandered down to the drinking fountain. She sipped at the cool water, then wiped the drips off her chin with the back of her hand. A few minutes later she went back to the office again, then dropped into the principal's leather chair and swung it around so she could look outside. The window faced a wooded park, and Jennie focused on a bed of flowers that circled one of the trees.

Although she tried not to think about what had happened, Jennie's curious nature kept asking questions. Who killed Mr. Mancini and why? Could the burglars have struck again? Had Mr. Mancini witnessed it? What if she had walked in a few minutes earlier—what would she have seen?

Her thoughts raced with possibilities. In one scenario the gunman turned on her as she opened the door. It gave her teacher the break he needed. He tackled the gunman. The gun went off and instead of the bullet striking Mr. Mancini it went straight into Jennie's heart.

"No." She shoved the disturbing scene aside. "It wouldn't have happened like that."

"Like what?"

Jennie whirled around in the chair, her heart hammering. "I—I didn't hear anyone come in. I was just thinking."

"Apparently." The man standing in front of the desk was tall and angular. His skin had the bronzed color of someone who spent a lot of time in the sun. He cleared his throat. "You must be Jennie McGrady. Officer Phelps told me I'd find you here."

She nodded. Her gaze drifted from his gray-streaked black hair and mustache to his nearly black eyes. He looked to be about Gram's age—maybe younger.

"I'm Lieutenant Rastovski." He raised his arm and set her book bag on the desk. "I believe this is yours."

Jennie smiled. "Yeah. Thanks. Rocky—um, Officer Rockwell—said I might not get it back for a while. Does this mean I'm in the clear?"

"Looks that way. From what we can determine so far, it looks like a suicide."

24

# 3

"Suicide? But that doesn't make sense. Why would he make an appointment with me, then kill himself?" Jennie tipped her head back against the chair.

The lieutenant shook his head. "Who knows? People do crazy things. Maybe he forgot he had an appointment."

Jennie doubted that. "Are you sure it was suicide? I mean, how can you tell?"

"He left a note, for one thing. The position of the body—and his gun. I won't go into details, but so far the evidence is consistent with a suicide."

"What about the noise I heard in the office?"

"Noise?"

"I told Officer Phelps about it. I was in the lab and heard something. I called out, but no one answered. Then I went to check. The outer door was open about six inches, but no one was there or in the parking lot."

The lieutenant frowned and tugged at the corner of his mustasche. "Could have been the wind."

"Maybe. There were some papers scattered on the floor. I picked them up," Jennie winced, then added, "but that was before I knew about the body. I do know better than to tamper with evidence."

"I see. Hopefully it won't matter in this case. The medical examiner's looking at suicide as well. Once she's done the autopsy we'll know for sure. Wish they were all this easy."

Call it a hunch, call it intuition, but something didn't feel right about labeling Mr. Mancini's death a suicide. She thought about enlightening the lieutenant, but doubted the guy would listen. And what did she know anyway? So she'd heard a noise. Jennie stared at Rastovski's striped tie. *The wind? Maybe.* A gust of wind could have scattered the papers on the floor. *Give it up, McGrady. Let the police do their job.*

"Can I go now?" Jennie glanced up to meet his eyes. He reminded her of someone—her cousin, Hazen White Cloud. She wondered if he might be of Indian or Spanish descent. Hazen was half Irish and half Nez Perce Indian. Lieutenant Rastovski looked like an older version and might even have been as handsome at one time. Now, though, his face had more of a rugged, lived-in look.

"We'll need to get prints so we can cross-check them with others we find at the crime scene, then you can go." The scar that ran along his jaw moved as he spoke.

Jennie found herself wondering how it happened. Law enforcement could be a dangerous business. For a moment her mind flickered back to her father. Was he still alive? Would anyone notify her if he'd been wounded? Jennie shook the macabre thoughts aside and focused back on what Rastovski had told her—something about fingerprints.

"You already have my prints on file."

His forehead creased in a disapproving frown. "Really."

"I've never been arrested, if that's what you're thinking. A few weeks ago my brother was kidnapped. The police fingerprinted all of us for comparison prints."

The lieutenant looked as if he meant to start questioning her all over again but only nodded. "Then you're free to go." He retrieved a business card from his shirt pocket and handed it to her. "Just in case you remember something or want to talk to me. I'll be in touch."

Jennie had almost made it to her car when a familiar bespectacled guy with a camera jogged toward her. "I might have known you'd be out here." She opened the door to the Mustang and tossed her bag in the backseat.

"I could say the same about you." Gavin Winslow—a skinny version of Clark Kent—grinned and raised his camera. "You must be the unidentified student the police were talking about."

"If I am, I'd just as soon stay that way." Jennie stuck her hand over the lens. "Come on, Gavin, give it a rest." Gavin worked as a part-time reporter at *The Oregonian*, Portland's primary newspaper. He was also a student at Trinity High and during the school year wrote and published the school paper.

"Sorry. Um, listen, I've got about all the dirt they're going to give me. I was hoping I could catch a ride back into town. Left my bike at the office." Gavin brushed a hand through his straight dark hair, drawing it off his forehead. His face was flushed and sweaty.

"How'd you get out here?"

"Hitched a ride with one of the other reporters." He shrugged. "The jerk left without me." Jennie sighed and looked at her watch. Two-thirty. She didn't want to drive back to Portland, especially with Gavin. He'd spend the entire time drilling her. What she really wanted to do was relax, swim a few laps, and laze in the sun. "I wasn't going home. I'm meeting Lisa over at Allison and B.J.'s. If you're not in a hurry you could come swimming with us and I could run you home after." She'd made the invitation knowing he wouldn't accept. Guilt slipped in and twisted at one of the knots still coiled in her stomach.

"I wish I could, but I gotta get back to the office." Gavin took a step back, looking like he'd been the last one picked for a baseball team. "Um—you go ahead. I'll see if I can find someone—"

"Okay, okay. I'll take you."

"Are you sure?" Without waiting for a response, he ran around to the passenger side of the car, yanked open the door, set his battered tan camera bag in the back, and folded his lanky form into the front seat. "I wouldn't want you to go out of your way."

"Yeah, right." Jennie winced as she came in contact with the hot black vinyl. "It's hot enough to bake bread in here."

Gavin wasn't listening. He read through the notes he'd taken on a steno pad, then wrote some more. Within a couple of minutes the air-conditioner had kicked in. Jennie ignored her passenger and concentrated on maneuvering around the empty police car that nearly blocked the driveway.

Once they were out on the main road, Gavin jotted the name Curtis Bolton off to the side of his notes and underlined it, then snapped the notebook closed. It was only then that Jennie realized he probably knew more about Mr. Mancini's death than she did.

"Did you get your story?" she asked.

"What?" he glanced at her, then back outside. "Oh yeah. I guess."

"Did you know him? Mr. Mancini, I mean."

Gavin nodded. "Some. Finished up the last couple weeks of chemistry with him. I questioned him last week about the break-in."

"And—"

"Nothing." He chewed on his bottom lip.

Jennie had a dozen questions but didn't ask them. Gavin didn't seem very talkative. She remembered something her grandmother had told her about getting people to open up. *"Let the silence work for you,"* Gram had said. *"Just listen and eventually they'll start talking."*

Gram was one of the wisest people Jennie knew. She'd retired from the police department a few years ago to become a travel writer. Gram did other things too, like occasionally working as a secret agent. Jennie made a mental note to call her later. She wanted to get Gram's views on the chemistry teacher's death. She also wanted to talk to Gram about Mom and Michael.

"They tell you it was a suicide?"

Gavin's question scattered her thoughts. She nodded.

"Hard to believe. I didn't know him all that well." Gavin tapped his pen against his note pad. "When we first got the call he'd been shot, I thought maybe it was related to that burglary."

"It still could be. They're not saying anything for sure yet." Jennie checked behind her for traffic, then eased onto the eastbound lanes of the Sunset Highway.

"True." He eyed her for a long moment. "So, what were you doing there, anyway?"

"I was supposed to have a meeting with Mr. Mancini to decide what I wanted to do for my project this quarter. I also wanted to set up a schedule. I had things pretty well worked out with Dr. Adams, but Mr. Mancini was having a hard time with my part-time status."

"I'm not surprised. The guy was totally inflexible. Did you ever meet him?"

"Just over the phone. He came in after I'd already finished my chemistry module. I left school a couple weeks early so I could go with Gram to Florida."

"Lucky you."

"Sounds as though you don't like him."

"We got along okay—but then, I like chemistry. Bolton and I are about the only two who did."

"Curtis Bolton? I noticed you wrote his name down in your notebook."

"He knew Mancini as well as anyone—thought I'd talk to him—see if he can shed any light on what happened." Gavin reached forward and turned the fan down a couple of notches. "Hope you don't mind. It's getting a little cool."

"No, we can shut it off and open the windows if you

want." He did. Jennie switched the lever to vent and cranked down her window.

The wind felt good whipping through her hair. If it hadn't been for Mr. Mancini she'd have rated the day a perfect ten. Sunshine, about 72 degrees, a slight breeze. The dark clouds of death had plunged it down to a two. She didn't want to think about Mr. Mancini, or why he'd killed himself, or why someone might have killed him.

Glancing over at her passenger, Jennie smiled. "Sure you don't want to go swimming?"

"I'd like to, but I have to finish up my story." He frowned, rubbed his forehead, and left his hand over his eyes. "I don't know if I can write this one, Jen. I'm a reporter, right? And I'm supposed to be objective—you know, detached. But I can't help thinking about him and wondering how he could have done something like that."

"Yeah, me too." Jennie hoped Gavin wasn't going to cry. She'd probably end up blubbering as well.

"Do you want to help me investigate?" Gavin asked.

"What?"

"I gotta know why he killed himself. What motivated him. Guys like Mancini don't commit suicide without a reason. And to use a gun. It's so messy. Besides, I still think there might be a connection to the burglary."

Jennie shook her head. "I'm sure the police will come up with an explanation."

"Yeah, right." Gavin turned to look out the window.

"I understand he left a note. Did they tell you what it said?"

"No."

"How come you're being so secretive?"

"How come you're asking so many questions? I thought you weren't interested."

"I'm curious. I want to know what's going on too."

He grinned. "I knew you couldn't resist. Maybe we can

get together after dinner and I'll show you what I've got so far."

"Call me first. Michael's coming over for dinner."

"You got it."

A few minutes later Jennie dropped Gavin off at *The Oregonian* and headed back out to the Lake Oswego area and the Beaumont Mansion. Not wanting to mull over the chemistry teacher's demise, she cranked the radio up and sang along with half a dozen contemporary artists. The songs didn't help. Maybe swimming would.

The Beaumont house sat back from the road, on a hill—like an elegant dollhouse on an expanse of plush green carpet. Driving up the long driveway Jennie waved at Manuel and his son, Rafael, who were weeding one of numerous rose gardens. The grounds keeper waved back. "*Hola*, Jennie," he called when she parked the car and got out. "The girls have been waiting for you. I have orders to tell you to go straight back to the pool."

"Thanks." Jennie paused on the way in to stick her nose into one of the fragrant salmon-colored blossoms that lined the walk.

When she looked up, Rafael glowered at her, and Jennie wondered what she'd done to deserve his anger. She didn't know him all that well. He and his mom and dad and four brothers and sisters had come from Mexico just a few weeks before. The Beaumonts were sponsoring them and had provided jobs and a home—the guest cottage behind the main house. Jennie thought about confronting him about his sullen attitude, then decided against it. Maybe he was just in a bad mood. Maybe he was jealous and would rather be swimming than pulling weeds. She could understand that.

Jennie grabbed her beach bag, let herself in, and hurried into the bathroom off the kitchen to change. The bathroom had two doors, the second of which led to the patio and pool area. Jennie pulled on her blue knit suit, hung her clothes on one of the many wooden hooks, and stepped outside.

"It's about time you got here." Lisa scrambled to her feet and hurried toward Jennie. "We heard about Mr. Mancini."

"I can't believe you were actually there." Allison stayed in her chair under the umbrella and, like the princess she was, waited for Jennie to reach her. Her sky-blue gaze traveled up to Jennie's face. "Are you okay?"

Jennie nodded. "I guess. How'd you hear about it so fast?"

"Michael called Dad." Allison tipped her head to one side to escape the sun, sending her straight, silky blond pageboy into motion. "Mom and Dad went to be with Mrs. Mancini and Alexis."

B.J., who'd been lying facedown on a chaise lounge, turned around and sat up, brushing damp curls out of her face. "So what gives, McGrady? You go in to question the new teach about the theft and he ends up dead."

Jennie sighed. "First of all, I didn't go in to question him. Secondly, I have no idea what gives." She eased into one of the white wrought-iron patio chairs, reached for the pitcher of pink lemonade, and snatched an empty glass from the tray. "I got there after it happened—at least I think so." After guzzling down half the lemonade and waiting for Lisa to sit, Jennie told the story the same way she'd told it to Officer Phelps and Lieutenant Rastovski.

"Any idea who might have killed him?" B.J. flipped a chair around and straddled it, draping her tan arms across the chairback.

"The police think he committed suicide."

"No kidding." B.J. whistled. "You just never know."

Lisa hugged herself. "I'm glad I didn't go with you."

Allison leaned forward, arms on the table. "It's just awful. I don't understand how someone could do that. I mean, think about his poor wife and Alex. They must be devastated."

"I doubt it." The sarcastic tone in B.J.'s voice brought Jennie up short.

"B.J., that's a terrible thing to say." Allison shot her younger sister a mind-your-manners look.

"Well, it's true. Which is why the suicide bit surprises me. Now, if you'd told me Mancini had been murdered, I wouldn't have any trouble believing it. And I can tell you, I'd put Alex and her mother right at the top of the suspect list." She dismounted the chair in much the same way one would get off a horse, walked over to the pool, and dove in.

# 4

"Honestly, Jennie, I don't know why B.J. would say something like that." Allison scowled at her sister's surfacing form. "Alex and Mrs. Mancini are both really nice people."

"Sounds like you know them pretty well."

"You could say that. Mrs. Mancini and our stepmom met at the Trinity women's retreat in June and really hit it off. They meet at the mall for lunch all the time, so Alex, B.J., and I hang out together—when we can get B.J. to come. You know how she hates to shop."

"Yeah, I know." Jennie glanced at Lisa and grinned. Lisa could relate all too well. Jennie wasn't crazy about the shopping thing either. Why shop when you didn't have money to buy anything? Of course these days B.J. had plenty of money. So did Jennie for that matter—not as much, but enough to put herself through college and law school. She'd been paid well for a couple of her crime-solving efforts. Still, old habits were hard to break. Besides, why spend money on stuff you didn't really need?

"Did you meet them, Lis?" Jennie asked.

Lisa shrugged. "At church. They seemed okay. Alex is a total snob, but other than that—"

"Lisa!" Allison swung around to object.

"Well, she is. She acts different to different people. She's nice to us—but I've seen the way she snubs some of the kids

34

at the mall—like she's too good to be seen with them."

Jennie sighed, then turning back to Allison, said, "Maybe B.J. saw some things you didn't. Anyway, we can talk about that later. I'm going for a swim."

Tossing her towel and watch on the nearest chaise lounge, Jennie walked to the edge of the Olympic-sized pool and watched her friend swim. Did B.J. actually know something about the situation, or was she just trying to goad them? Jennie had a hunch B.J.'s and Lisa's assessments were closer to the truth than Allison's. Not that Allison would lie—she just tended to overlook the darker side of life. Probably because, unlike B.J., she'd never seen much of it.

The sisters were about as different as siblings could get. Part of that was personality, but a lot had to do with how they were raised. They were victims of divorce. The first Mrs. Beaumont had run off when Allison was a year old. What she never bothered to tell Allison's dad was that she was pregnant. B.J. never knew about her dad and sister until her mom died and a social worker found a birth certificate. B.J. had spent most of her fifteen years trying to survive, sometimes even living on the streets and going hungry. Allison had always had everything she needed and more. Jennie tended to trust B.J.'s instincts—especially since they often mirrored her own.

Jennie climbed on the diving board, reached the end in two strides, and dove in. For a few heavenly moments, the cool, clear water washed away the awful sense of being held prisoner. By what, Jennie didn't know. She hadn't even been able to put a name to the oppressive feelings until now. She surfaced, hauled in air, swam ten lengths of the pool, then stopped at the shallow end to catch her breath. *You're out of shape, McGrady.*

"You going to be on the swim team again this year?" B.J. splashed up to Jennie and hoisted herself out of the pool, then sat on the edge, dangling her feet in the water.

"Probably."

"So am I."

Jennie grinned. "Really? Coach Dayton got to you, huh?"

"No, I just decided you needed a little competition."

Jennie backed away from the side and sent a wall of water flying in B.J.'s direction. She hit her target and then some. Lisa shrieked as the cool water hit her sun-warmed back. "I'll get you for that." Lisa hit the tile running and cannonballed into the pool.

Their horseplay took on a serious note when B.J. suggested volleyball. They strung a net across the pool and paired off, Jennie and Lisa against Allison and B.J.

Some time later, Jennie climbed out of the pool to check the time. "Oh, wow, it's five-thirty," she moaned. "Mom's going to kill me. I was supposed to be home by five."

"I'd better go too." Lisa slipped a matching skirt over her swimsuit. The neon tropical fish on her skirt came to life as she towel dried her hair.

Jennie pulled an oversized T-shirt on over her suit, slipped on sandals, and scurried into the bathroom to get her clothes. After giving Mom a call to say she was on her way home, Jennie and her cousin said their goodbyes and walked out to their cars.

"What are you going to do now?" Lisa asked.

"Go home."

"No, I mean about Mr. Mancini."

"Nothing." Jennie opened the door of her Mustang and turned to face Lisa. "I know that seems strange coming from me, but I don't want to know what happened to Mr. Mancini. I don't want to think about it."

"Really got to you, didn't it?"

Jennie swallowed back an unexpected flow of tears. "Yeah, I guess it did."

"I'm sorry I brought it up."

"It's okay. Um—we'll talk later, okay? I gotta get home

before Mom decides to ground me for the next six months."

"Okay, I'll see you later." Lisa's green gaze drifted from Jennie's face back toward the house. She smiled, her already flushed cheeks glowing brighter.

Jennie turned to see what or who she was looking at. "Rafael?" The gardener leaned on the hoe and watched them. His mood apparently hadn't improved.

"Isn't he a hunk? I thought Brad was cute, but Rafael is— I don't know. So mysterious and—" She sighed and had that dreamy look in her eyes Jennie recognized all too well.

"I thought you were giving Brad another chance." Brad had been Lisa's boyfriend most of the summer.

Lisa wrinkled her freckled nose. "We broke up—it was mutual."

"So, have you and Rafael gone out?"

"Not yet. I keep hoping he'll ask. I think he wants to, but for some reason . . ."

"Maybe he's embarrassed. I mean, he's a gardener and you're the boss's daughter's friend. That could be intimidating."

"That shouldn't matter. I think he's just shy."

"So go talk to him."

Lisa grinned. "You sound just like B.J. Maybe I will." Instead of getting into the car, Lisa started back toward the garden. "Wish me luck."

"As if you need it," Jennie murmured. Lisa had no trouble getting guys. She was cute and bubbly and sweet and altogether a very nice person.

Jennie put the towel over the black vinyl, tossed in her beach bag, folded herself into the car, and drove off. Normally it took twenty minutes to make the drive from the Lake Oswego area where the Beaumonts and Lisa lived to the Crystal Lake area on the east side of the Willamette River. Normally. Rush-hour traffic slowed her to a crawl, and the commute took over an hour.

By the time she finally got home, Mom and Michael were clearing off the dinner dishes. After the grueling drive, the last thing Jennie needed was a lecture on the importance of being on time, but that's what she got. Thanks to Michael, it was a shortened version.

"Being late was bad enough, Jennie," Mom said as she neared the end of her speech. "What really upsets me is that you didn't call me."

"I did—from Allison's."

"I'm talking about the incident at the school. My daughter and fiancé find a . . ." She glanced down at Nick and spelled b-o-d-y. ". . . and I have to hear about it on the news."

"Honey, I told you I was sorry. I should have called." Michael slipped an arm around Mom's shoulders. "It's just that with all the meetings and arrangements . . ."

Mom folded her arms and stepped away from him. "I don't want to hear any excuses from either of you." She grabbed a platter of leftover salmon from the table and headed for the kitchen. "Jennie, I'll leave the food out. Fix yourself a plate. When you've finished eating you can do the dishes."

Michael and Jennie looked at each other. He had a kind of what-do-I-do-now look on his face and Jennie felt sorry for him. But not sorry enough to reassure him. For a moment Jennie found herself hoping maybe he'd change his mind about marrying Mom. "What can I say? Mom's got a terrible temper."

"I know." He smiled. "But she's beautiful when she's mad."

Jennie rolled her eyes and headed for the kitchen. People in love were hopeless.

Having worked up an appetite swimming, Jennie piled her plate with grilled salmon, wild rice, and green beans, covered it, and set it in the microwave to heat. While she waited, she finished off the remaining Caesar salad and set the bowl on the counter next to the sink. She ate dinner alone. Well, not quite. She could hear Michael reading to Nick in the other room. Bernie, Nick's St. Bernard puppy, looked bored as he ambled into the kitchen. He sat quietly beside her stool and watched her eat, his sad brown eyes filled with longing.

"Don't look at me like that," she said. "I can't feed you. Dogs aren't supposed to have fish—too many bones."

He whimpered.

"Hey, I'm sorry. I don't make the rules."

"Woof." He wagged his tail and lifted his left paw, then tapped Jennie's foot.

"You don't make it easy, do you?" She broke off a piece of salmon and, after checking it carefully for bones, surrendered the delicate pink morsel. Bernie gently licked it off her hand, then sat back down.

Six bites later Jennie held up her empty hands. "That's it. All gone." With Bernie still looking for a handout, she gathered her dishes and took them to the sink.

She'd almost finished the dishes when the phone rang. "I'll get it." Jennie half expected it to be Lisa calling to say she was going out with Rafael. Maybe that's why she didn't recognize the voice at first.

"Jennie, this is Maddie Winslow, Gavin's mom."

"Oh, hi, Mrs. Winslow. How's it going?"

"All right. Is Gavin there? He hasn't come home and I'm getting worried."

"No. I haven't seen him since this afternoon. I dropped him off at *The Oregonian* around three." Jennie tucked the phone between her chin and shoulder and began washing off the counter.

"His boss said he left there at four-thirty. I don't know where else to call."

"Did you try Courtney's?" Courtney Evans was Gavin's girlfriend.

"She's working and hasn't seen him all day. I sent his dad out to check the roads. I hate having him ride his bike in all that traffic."

It was a long way from downtown Portland to the Winslows' farm in east county. "I'm sure he's okay, Mrs. Winslow. He may still be working on the story about Mr. Mancini."

"Oh yes. Wasn't that awful? I don't know what the world's coming to. Well, I won't keep you. If you hear from Gavin, tell him to call me."

Jennie promised she would and hung up.

After finishing her kitchen chores, Jennie headed into the living room. Apparently Mom and Michael had made up. They were snuggled together watching television. Nick had fallen asleep on Michael's lap.

"Who was on the phone, honey?" Mom had apparently forgiven her too.

"Maddie Winslow. She was looking for Gavin."

Mom twisted around to look at her. "Oh, he called earlier. Around six. I'm sorry, with dinner and everything, I forgot."

"Where is he? What did he want?"

"Just wanted you to call him. Something about a major breakthrough."

"Did he leave a number?"

"It's on the pad by the phone."

Back in the kitchen, Jennie tore the number off the scratch pad, then raced upstairs to her private phone. She punched out the numbers thinking they seemed familiar. After a couple of rings an answering machine came on. "You have reached the offices of Trinity High School. Our office hours are—"

Jennie hung up. Her stomach tied itself in at least a dozen knots. She set the scrap of paper beside the phone and sank onto her bed. Why had Gavin called from the school at that time of night? How could he have gotten in?

She didn't want to think the worst, but what could she do? Her mind kept digging up bits and pieces that seemed to form a dark and frightening picture. The theft at the school, Rocky's warning about clandestine labs, Gavin's snoopy nature, and Mr. Mancini's death.

Gavin Winslow was in trouble.

# 5

*Okay, McGrady. Just calm down.* If Gavin was at the school office he couldn't have been alone. Maybe Mrs. Talbot had stayed late. Jennie pulled out the school directory and called Mrs. Talbot. No answer. After leaving a message on the machine, she ran back downstairs to talk to Michael and nearly collided with him on the stairs. He and Mom were bringing Nick up to bed.

Nick, head on Michael's shoulder, yawned and reached for Jennie. "You were s'posed to show me the pictures."

Jennie brushed a lock of dark hair from his forehead and kissed him on the nose. "Too late tonight, Buddy. We'll look at them tomorrow."

Surprisingly, he didn't argue.

"Michael, I need to talk to you," she whispered and followed them to Nick's room.

After settling Nick onto the bed, Mom stayed to get Nick into his pajamas. Michael came back into the hall. "What's going on? You look worried."

"I am—about Gavin." She explained the phone message and added, "I thought maybe you'd seen him."

Michael shook his head. "He shouldn't have been in the school. Mrs. Talbot left at four-thirty. Unless someone with a key was with him he couldn't have gotten in without setting off the alarm."

42

"Could he have gotten a key?"

"Not likely. I'd better make some calls. He may have met someone there."

Jennie nodded. "While you're doing that I'll call his mom."

Back in her room, Jennie looked up Gavin's number. As it rang, she closed her eyes. *Oh, please God, let him be home. Please.*

"Hello!"

Jennie could tell by the worried note in Mrs. Winslow's voice that Gavin hadn't come back. She took a deep breath and told her about Gavin's phone call.

"I don't understand why he'd give you the number at the school. How could he have gotten in? I'm sure Mrs. Talbot leaves around four."

"Actually, she went home at four-thirty. I talked to Michael and he's calling some of the other staff members. I thought you should know."

"Thank you. Um—could you let me know if Michael finds anything? Maybe I'll call Mrs. Talbot at home. She could have gone back—"

"I already did. There's no answer." An image of the secretary and Gavin lying dead in the school office slammed into her mind. Jennie willed it to go away. *Stop it, McGrady. You've been reading too many mysteries. It didn't happen.* But it could have.

"I suppose it's too soon to call the police."

Jennie didn't know what to tell her. "Um—maybe we should wait and see what Michael finds out."

"Yes. I'll do that. Thank you."

After hanging up, Jennie went back downstairs. She found Michael in the living room, phone in hand. "I see: Okay, thanks. Yeah, I'll let you know."

"Did you find out anything?" Jennie asked when he hung up.

"No one's seen him, and all the keys are accounted for except Mrs. Talbot's and Tom Mancini's. The police should have Mr. Mancini's."

"What about Mrs. Talbot? Any idea where she might be?"

"No. She was still pretty shaken over Mancini's death when she left. Might have gone to a friend's."

"Or she might be at the school." The horrible images of Mrs. Talbot and Gavin hovered again in the periphery of her mind. "I think we should drive over there and take a look around."

"Might not be a bad idea."

"Drive over where?" Mom's gaze darted from Michael to Jennie. "What's going on?"

"Gavin Winslow hasn't been home this evening and Mrs. Talbot isn't home," Michael answered. "That number he gave you was for the school."

"Have you thought about calling the police to check things out?"

Michael ran a hand through his hair. "Yes. But I hate to involve them unnecessarily."

"Unnecessarily?" Mom heaved a deep sigh. "Let me get this straight. You've had burglary—and a suicide—and now Gavin is missing? What are you waiting for?"

Michael frowned. "Susan, please try to understand. We've been getting a lot of bad press lately. Our attendance is down. We just can't afford to have the papers running more negative stories about the school. I'm just going to run over and see if everything is okay."

"All right, fine. Do what you have to do."

"Thanks, Mom. We won't be too long."

"Hold it!" Mom grabbed Jennie's arm. "You're not going anywhere."

"But Gavin—"

"No."

"Your mother's right, Jennie."

44

"But you said—"

"I said it was a good idea. For me—not for you." He grabbed his keys off the dining room table. "I'll call."

"Michael." Mom stopped him at the door. "Be careful."

Michael nodded, then folded her into his arms and kissed her. Jennie plodded into the living room and flopped into the recliner.

A few seconds later she heard the front door close. Mom walked into the living room, picked up the cups they'd left on the coffee table, and went into the kitchen.

Jennie waited for her mother to join her and deliver another lecture. Seven minutes passed and Mom still hadn't come back. Curious, Jennie unfolded her arms and headed into the dining room. She stopped when she reached the entry to the kitchen.

Mom was sitting at the table reading. Beside her Bible and devotional book sat a large chocolate brownie with whipped topping and a cup of tea. A second brownie and teacup sat in front of an empty chair. Jennie's annoyance faded into a smile. She should have known.

"I was about to start without you." Mom closed her Bible, set it to the side, and pulled the cream-topped brownie toward her.

"Yeah, right. I'll bet you already had one." Jennie drew out the chair next to Mom and sat down.

Mom smiled. "I did—after dinner."

"What kind of tea did you make?" Jennie lifted the cosy off the teapot and poured the greenish liquid into her cup.

"Your favorite."

Jennie held the cup to her lips and sipped. As the delicate peppermint scent drifted into her nostrils, she felt herself relax. Of all the traditions Gram had passed down to her family, this was the best. *Tea quiets the soul*, Gram would tell them. And it did. Over the years they'd solved a lot of problems over tea.

"You've had a rough day." Mom picked up her fork and scooped up a dollop of whipped topping.

Jennie sighed. "Yeah." She speared a piece of the moist brownie and popped it into her mouth, then ate several more bites before speaking again.

"Mom—"

"Jennie—" They both spoke at once and laughed at each other.

"You go first," Mom said.

"I just wanted to tell you I'm sorry about not getting home on time and for not calling you about Mr. Mancini. What were you going to say?"

"Just that I'm sorry too. I should have been more understanding. I didn't know about your teacher until I watched the five-o'clock news and couldn't believe it. And to have you both involved—I'm not sure who I was more angry with, you or Michael. Then when you didn't come home . . ."

"I don't know why I didn't call you. I guess I kind of thought Michael had. When it first happened he called the police, then Beaumonts'. I thought he called you too. Guess I should have asked."

"Hmm." Mom finished a mouthful of brownie, then asked, "Do you feel like talking about it?"

"What?"

"Mr. Mancini. It must have been terrible for you. Michael said you felt guilty you didn't find him first and that you were thinking you might have been able to help."

"I did. I still do." Jennie set her fork down.

"Oh, sweetheart." Mom reached for Jennie's hand. "From what Michael told me, Mr. Mancini had to have died instantly."

Jennie brought the cup to her lips and let the soothing tea warm her insides. "I can't stop thinking about it. It's like this voice inside me keeps telling me to—"

"To what, Jennie?"

46

*To keep looking. To find out what really happened.* Jennie kept the thought to herself. Mom wouldn't understand. "I just can't let it go."

Mom nodded. "Give it time, honey. You've had a traumatic experience. Might even want to see Gloria."

Jennie didn't answer. Gloria was one of the counselors at Trinity Center. She'd helped Jennie deal with Mom's decision to get a divorce and date Michael. She doubted the counselor could help much in this case. What Jennie needed most at the moment were a few answers—and to know Gavin was safe.

"Would you like me to make an appointment?"

"Uh—no. I'll be fine."

"Okay, but if you change your mind . . ."

Jennie glanced at the digital green numbers of the microwave. Ten o'clock. Michael should have been there by now. She chewed on her bottom lip wondering what he'd find there. Needing to change the subject, she asked Mom about the wedding. "So, have you two set a date? I sort of thought that was what tonight's dinner was about."

"It was. Only we didn't get a chance to discuss it." She pressed her fork down on the plate to gather the crumbs. "After I blew up at him today, he'll probably call the whole thing off."

"I doubt it. He thinks you're beautiful when you're angry."

Mom's green eyes brightened. "He said that? How sweet."

*Oh, Mom,* Jennie longed to say. *Don't marry Michael. He loves you, but so does Dad. Dad is alive, Mom, and someday maybe he'll be able to come home. It's too dangerous right now, but . . .* It just wasn't right. The government should have told Mom the truth. Dad should find a way to let her know.

The phone rang. Jennie shot out of her chair and grabbed it before it could ring a second time. "Michael?"

"Um, no, this is Rocky."

"Oh, hi." The race for the phone had left her breathless.

"I hope I'm not calling too late. I just got off work and wanted to see how you were holding up."

"Okay. Did you find out anything more about Mr. Mancini's death?"

"It's looking more and more like a suicide. There was gunpowder residue on his hands. And it looks like he may have been taking crank."

"What?"

"The story'll be in the paper tomorrow morning. The medical examiner says he was using some kind of methamphetamine. Found a syringe in the office waste basket under a bunch of papers. We figure he might have been the one who stole the supplies from the lab."

"That's awful. Are you sure?"

"It's not my call. Just talked to Lieutenant Rastovski. He's hoping to close the case soon."

"So it was suicide. I wonder if that's why Gavin called."

"You kids aren't playing private detective again are you?"

"No. Not exactly. I mean—Gavin might have been investigating the theft." Jennie briefly filled him in on the conversation she'd had earlier with Gavin.

"Gavin is missing and no one bothered to call us?"

"Michael wanted to see if he could find him first."

"I'm on my way home. I'll drive around out by the school, see what I can find out. Give me Winslow's address, and I'll ask someone to check around out there as well. Normally it would be too soon for his parents to file a missing-persons report, but considering the circumstances I feel like we should investigate."

Jennie thanked him and had just hung up when the phone rang again. This time it was Michael calling from the school. "We didn't find him. I called Maddie and she still hasn't seen him."

"I just talked to Rocky, he should be there in a few minutes. Could you tell if Gavin had been there?"

When Michael hesitated, Jennie's stomach tightened. "You found something."

"His bike. Found it parked in the faculty parking lot next to Mancini's car."

# 6

"It's my fault." Jennie sat at the kitchen table, her head buried in her arms. "If I'd been paying attention to the time, I wouldn't have been late. I wouldn't have gotten stuck in traffic." She paused to blow her nose. "I should have been here when he called. . . ."

"Sweetheart, you couldn't have known." Mom laid her hand on Jennie's arm. "Right now I'm glad you *were* late. If you'd gone to meet him, you might be missing as well."

"But I could have talked to him—found out what he was doing at the school. At least I'd have some names. I'd know what he wanted to tell me."

Jennie took a deep, shuddering breath. *Crying isn't doing you any good at all, McGrady. Just stop whining and do something.* A police officer would be coming to question her any minute. She had to pull herself together.

After washing her face, she felt better. Jennie hated crying and avoided it whenever possible. Tears left her face all splotchy, but she couldn't help it. Hearing about Gavin had triggered a landslide of the stuff that had been building all day.

The doorbell rang. Jennie pressed a cool washcloth to her eyes one more time, then dried her hands and face before making her way downstairs.

Officer Phelps stood in the entry talking to Mom. "Sorry

50

to bother you this late, ma'am, but I'll need to ask you and your daughter some questions about the Winslow boy."

"Of course, but I'm not sure we'll be much help, though. Come in." Mom led the way into the living room. "Would you like to sit down?"

"Thank you, but that won't be necessary." The officer pulled a black notebook out of her back pocket and flipped it open. She was as officious as she had been at the school.

"Can I get you coffee or anything?" Mom offered.

"I'm fine, thank you. I understand Gavin called here around six." Phelps didn't look fine. Jennie noted the lines under her eyes. Apparently it had been a long day for her as well.

Mom gave her the information. "That's all I can tell you, I'm afraid."

Phelps leveled a cool gaze on Jennie. "When did you last see him?"

"Um—this afternoon—after I left the school. He needed a ride downtown so I dropped him off." Jennie had a distinct feeling the officer didn't like her, but she couldn't imagine why.

"Did he give you any indication he'd be going back out to the school?"

"No. He just asked me if I wanted to help him investigate."

"Investigate what?"

Jennie frowned. "The burglary and Mr. Mancini's death. He thought they might be related."

"And what did you tell him?"

Jennie squirmed under the officer's condemning gaze. "I really wasn't planning to get involved in the case—especially after Rocky told me about the drug labs."

"By Rocky, I assume you mean Officer Rockwell?" Phelps glanced up from her note taking.

Jennie nodded.

"Is this Winslow kid your boyfriend?"

"No. Just a friend. My boyfriend is in Alaska—fishing. But then, you don't need to know that, do you?"

"Not unless he's missing too."

Though she hadn't heard from Ryan in a while, Jennie didn't think he was and told Officer Phelps as much.

A tiny grin escaped the stern officer's lips until she pressed them together.

The questioning over, Officer Phelps left. Mom straightened the throw pillows on the couch and slipped an arm around Jennie's waist. "We'd better get some rest."

Jennie, being nearly a head taller, rested her cheek on Mom's hair. "I'll never be able to sleep."

"Then just close your eyes." They walked arm in arm through the dining room and up the stairs.

"Is Michael coming back tonight?"

"No. He called while you were upstairs. He's going out to the Winslows' to lend some moral support."

"That's good. Maddie must be frantic by now."

"I imagine so." Mom passed by Jennie's room and stopped at Nick's door. "I'd better check on him—he's been rather troubled for the last few days." She frowned. "Jennie, have you been talking to Nick about your father possibly coming home again?"

"No. How could I? He asked me about Dad this morning, though. Seems to be worried about having two dads."

"Yes. He mentioned that to me as well. I haven't told him, you know. About Jason being dead. I'm not sure I want to yet. I thought I'd wait another year. On the other hand I don't want to encourage him either. Tonight he wanted to go to sleep with his real dad's picture instead of Coco bear and his blanket."

Jennie shrugged. "Nick isn't stupid, Mom. He knows Michael isn't his real dad. Maybe he feels like he's betraying Dad by loving Michael. Today I told him Dad would under-

52

stand and that since he couldn't be with us he'd want Nick to have a stepdad like Michael."

"Did you?" Mom smiled. "That was very nice of you."

"Thanks. Good night, Mom. I love you." Jennie ducked into her room before she said something she shouldn't—couldn't—say.

As she often did when she was anxious or nervous, Jennie paced. Pausing at her desk, she picked up a multicolor glass paperweight. She stared into the swirling shades of crimson and blue. Random patterns. Gram and J.B. had brought it back from Europe several weeks before. Austrian crystal. Jennie set the paperweight down and tried calling her grandmother. As was so often the case lately, no one was home. Not even the answering machine picked up.

She dialed Lisa's number, but the line was busy.

Jennie changed into her pajamas—a cotton T-shirt tie-dyed in shades of blue and matching shorts. For the next hour or so, she wrote in her diary, which consisted mainly of letters to her father. She hadn't written a letter to him in a long time—not since she discovered he was still alive.

> *Dear Dad,*
>
> *I'm feeling pretty rotten right now. My friend Gavin is missing—not officially, of course, but at least the cops are taking it seriously. I'm worried that it might have something to do with Mr. Mancini's death. Police think he committed suicide. I'm having trouble with that. Gavin did too. Maybe that's why he's missing.*
>
> *There may be drugs involved. That's a scary thought. I wish you could be here to handle it. That's your specialty, right? Do you ever think about working in the States? I suppose it's not as exciting as being in the tropics, but wouldn't you be safer? By the way, Mom and Michael are back together again and talking marriage—like really soon. . . .*

Jennie continued to write, telling him about Montana and getting to know Mom's sister Maggie and her twin cousins, Heather and Hazen, and their little sister, Amber. Thinking about them spurred her to write a letter to them too. At least she could mail that one. Maybe she'd write a letter to Hannah as well, to thank her for the locket.

It was midnight before Jennie finally crawled into bed. Trying to keep her mind from dwelling on all the terrible things that could have happened to Gavin, she started reading a new mystery. Unfortunately, she couldn't concentrate on the story. At twelve-thirty she set the book aside, closed her eyes, and said a prayer for Gavin and his family, and for the Mancinis.

As she drifted into sleep, Jennie felt herself falling. Something or someone was pulling her into a deep, dark, frightening place. She fought against it, but the force was too great and she finally let go.

————

Birds chirping outside her window and the sun peeking through the blinds urged Jennie awake. She stretched and yawned as bits and pieces of the day before settled into place. The anxious feeling that had gone to bed for the night crept back into her stomach. Jennie tossed the covers aside and padded across the plush carpet to the window seat. Moving a couple of her stuffed bears to one side, she sat on the wide cushioned bench and raised the blinds, then leaned back and let the sun melt away the chill she felt inside.

Was Gavin still missing? Part of her wanted to run downstairs to find out. Another part didn't want to know. Finally, unable to stand not knowing, Jennie left her cozy perch. She found her mother at the kitchen table, drinking coffee and reading the paper.

Jennie kissed Mom's cheek. "Where's Nick?"

"Still sleeping."

"Have you heard anything about Gavin?"

Mom shook her head and set her mug on the table. "Michael called a few minutes ago. Other than the bike and helmet, they haven't found any sign of him."

*No news is good news,* Jennie reminded herself while she fixed a bowl of granola and blueberry yogurt and sat down at the table. She hoped the adage held true.

"The police haven't declared him officially missing yet," Mom went on. "It hasn't been twenty-four hours."

"How's Mrs. Winslow doing?"

"Worried, of course. I'm going out there as soon as Nick gets up—do you want to come along?"

"Um—no. I think I'll hang around here—maybe clean my room and head over to Lisa's later. I tried calling Gram last night. Are she and J.B. still in town?"

"I think so. They said something about going back to the coast today, though."

"So soon? I hardly ever get to see her since she married J.B." Gram had been busy before, but being married to an FBI agent tended to complicate things even more. "I miss her."

"I know you do. Maybe you can go down to the coast and stay for a week or so before school starts."

"I'd love that!" Despite the seriousness of the situation with Gavin and Mr. Mancini, Jennie's spirits took an upward turn. Ryan would be home soon, and since he was Gram's next-door neighbor, she'd be able to spend some time with him as well.

"I'm going to shower and get Nick up. Could you take care of Bernie?"

"Sure."

Mom dumped the remains of her coffee in the sink, rinsed the cup, and left. Jennie finished her cereal, downed a glass of juice, then went out to the back porch.

"Hi, big guy," Jennie cooed as she hunkered down to pet

Bernie. "You don't like being out here away from all of us, do you?"

Bernie whined and stretched up to lick Jennie's face. When they'd first gotten the St. Bernard he'd been allowed to sleep and eat in the house. Now Mom said he was too big. So, Michael and Nick built a doghouse and moved him out to the back porch.

After giving him fresh water and a mountain of dog food, Jennie hurried upstairs to shower and dress.

At ten o'clock Mom and Nick waved goodbye, leaving Jennie with requests to do the breakfast dishes and vacuum. Lisa drove in as they were leaving.

Lisa looked anything but pleased as she climbed out of the maroon Ford Taurus and joined Jennie on the front porch. "I can't believe you didn't call me when you found out about Gavin."

"I tried, but your line was busy."

"Oh." Her freckled cheeks flushed bright pink. "I was talking to Rafael. Mom says I shouldn't be calling him. She thinks I should wait until he makes the first move. But that's dumb. I mean, it's okay for girls to call guys." She shrugged her shoulders. "Anyway, it didn't do much good. He still didn't ask me out. I may have to ask him. Do you think I'm being too pushy?"

"You're asking me? You're the expert on guys. Anyway, I wouldn't worry about it. He'll come around." Jennie followed her cousin inside and closed the door. "So how did you find out about Gavin?"

"Mom told me this morning. I guess Mrs. Winslow called her late last night to see if we'd seen him. They must have called everyone they could think of. That is so scary. I hope they find him soon."

"Me too." Jennie opened the hall closet and pulled out the upright vacuum cleaner. "I have to do some housework. Want to help?"

"No, but I will."

Jennie sent Lisa into the kitchen while she straightened the living room, dusted, and vacuumed. She wanted to be out looking for Gavin but had no idea where to begin. Maybe she'd call Rocky and the Winslows later and get an official update.

Lisa wandered in from the kitchen just as Jennie was putting the vacuum cleaner away. She was munching on an apple and reading a section of newspaper.

"Did you see this?"

"What?" Jennie closed the hall closet door and looked over her cousin's shoulder.

"This article about Mr. Mancini." Lisa handed her the paper and shuddered. "It is just so gruesome. If I were going to kill myself, which I'd never do, I wouldn't use a gun—especially if I had drugs around. I mean, wouldn't it have been more efficient, not to mention less messy, to take an overdose?"

"Good question. Be quiet for a minute and let me read it." The headline declared the teacher's death a suicide. Jennie didn't recognize the name under the title and wondered what had happened to Gavin's story. There were no surprises in the first few paragraphs. As Rocky had told her the night before, the police suspected drug use had contributed to the teacher's decision to end his life in such a violent way.

The article went on to tell how Mr. Mancini's body had been discovered by an unidentified student and the youth pastor at the adjoining church. The reporter had interviewed Mrs. Mancini, Michael, Mrs. Talbot, and several others including Mr. Mancini's current lab assistant, Curtis Bolton. They all shared the same kind of shock and disbelief.

As she read, she began thinking in terms of talking to these people herself, especially Mrs. Mancini and Curtis Bolton. Of course she'd never met Mrs. Mancini, but she vaguely knew Curtis and wasn't surprised at his being the new lab assistant. He tended to be a loner—quiet and shy—a four-point student who'd end up being a college professor, an inventor, or a rocket scientist someday. He was kind of cute in a studious sort of way, straw-colored hair, gangly arms and legs that didn't go with the rest of his body.

"Lisa, what do you know about Curtis Bolton? It says here he's Mr. Mancini's lab assistant."

"He's super intelligent and comes from a very wealthy family. I think they live out in east county—near the Winslows." Lisa pinched her eyes closed as if that might help her memory. "He has a brother—Ray—and a married sister who lives in California."

"How do you remember all that?"

"They were at church a couple of weeks ago and Pastor Dave congratulated Ray on graduating from Oregon State. After church I talked to him and his brother."

"And . . ."

"Nothing. I invited Curtis to come to our youth meetings when they start up in the fall, and he said he'd think about it."

Jennie scanned the rest of the article, then went back and reread the part about the suicide note.

"This is strange."

"What's that?" Lisa grabbed hold of the paper and pulled it toward her.

"This article says Mr. Mancini had left a suicide note on his computer, but he couldn't have. I was in his office. The only thing I saw on his computer was some kind of chemical equation or formula. Definitely not a suicide note."

"Maybe the paper made a mistake or someone gave them the wrong information."

"I need to find out for sure."

"Does it matter all that much?"

"Of course it does. Don't you see? If the police found a suicide note on the computer it had to have been written after

I left the office. That means Mr. Mancini didn't write it."
Jennie frowned. "Unless I was wrong about his being dead
before I got there."

"What did the note say?" Lisa asked.

"I thought you read it."

"Not completely."

Jennie began reading. *"For Sandra and Alex and my good
friends at Trinity, when you find this note I'll be gone. I can no
longer live with the shame of what I have done. Please forgive me.
You and the school will be better off without me. Tom Mancini."*

"Wait a minute." Lisa grabbed hold of the paper. "Read
that again."

"Why, what's wrong?"

Lisa pointed to the first line. "It says, 'for Alex.' "

"That's his daughter, right?"

"Jennie, you're right. Mr. Mancini didn't write this note."

"How can you tell?"

"The only people who call her Alex are her friends. She
told me Mr. Mancini hated that name. He made it a point to
always call her Alexis."

# 7

"I need to talk to Lieutenant Rastovski." Jennie set the paper on the table, then went in search of her book bag. After several minutes of pawing through miscellaneous scraps of paper in her wallet, she found the card he'd given her.

The operator transferred the call to the lieutenant, whose voice mail told her he wasn't available and to leave a message. Jennie did, then called again and this time asked for Rocky.

"Officer Rockford is on patrol," the woman answering the phone told her. "If this is an emergency you'll need to call 9-1-1."

"No, it isn't, but I need to talk to him or Lieutenant Rastovski as soon as possible—I have some information about the Mancini case."

"I see. Lieutenant Rastovski is tied up in a meeting this morning. But I'll see that he gets your message."

"When will he be free?"

"By noon, I expect."

Jennie gave her name and number and hung up. Frustrated, she stuffed the card in the pocket of her jeans and turned back to Lisa. "No one's ever around when you need them. Looks like Rastovski won't be in for another hour."

Lisa retrieved a Diet Coke from the refrigerator. "Want one?"

"I guess."

She pulled out another one along with a tray of ice from the freezer and set them on the counter. "Want yours in a glass?"

"Yep." Jennie leaned against the counter and watched her. Lisa's resemblance to Mom always amazed Jennie. Jennie had the McGrady genes—dark hair and eyes. She took after Gram, Dad, and Lisa's mother, Kate, who was Dad's twin sister. Lisa, on the other hand, took after the Calhoun side of the family, with their red hair and freckles. Mom was Lisa's dad's sister, so she was a Calhoun too. It was all very complicated and it really didn't matter all that much. They were all one big happy family—most of the time. Which explained why Lisa was as much at home in the McGrady kitchen as Jennie.

"Thanks," Jennie said when Lisa handed her a glass. "Want to wait out on the porch? It should be shady by now."

"I guess."

Jennie carried their drinks out to the front porch and set them on the white wicker table. The screen door squeaked and banged shut.

She stretched out on the porch swing, left leg dangling, and watched a squirrel scurry up a nearby tree. A patrol car cruised up to the curb and stopped. *Rocky.* Jennie scrambled to her feet and met him halfway up the walk. "Hi. I didn't think you'd get my message so quickly."

"What message? I came by to see if you'd heard from your friend."

"Unfortunately no, but I left a call for you." Jennie explained how she and Lisa had found the discrepancies in the suicide note.

"Hmm. Interesting observation, but I didn't see the note. You need to talk to Lieutenant Rastovski. He'll be able to answer your questions better than I can."

"Do you think he'll listen? I mean he seemed pretty sure it was suicide."

"Makes it a whole lot easier for the department if it is. Rastovski's got a case load like you wouldn't believe."

Rocky's radio emitted static along with a series of words and numbers that apparently meant something to him. He mumbled into the transmitter, told Jennie he'd talk to her later, then left.

After Jennie and Lisa had drained their drinks, Jennie had had it with waiting around. "I'm going down there."

"To the police department?"

"It could be hours before Rastovski calls me back. I want to try to catch him when he gets out of his meeting."

Lisa glanced at her watch. "I have to go. Allison and B.J. and I might go to the mall. Besides, if I hurry I can get to their house in time to watch Rafael clean the pool."

"Clean the—Lisa, that is so tacky." Jennie picked up their glasses and Lisa's plate.

"No it isn't." Lisa held open the door and followed Jennie inside. "We have it all planned. We'll swim for a while, and then Allison and B.J. will go inside. I'll say I want to get in a couple more laps. I am supposed to be exercising, you know, and I'll just happen to be in the pool when he comes to clean it. We'll talk for a few minutes and—" She shrugged. "Who knows."

Jennie shook her head. She had long ago given up trying to understand how she and Lisa could be so different when it came to guys. Lisa was so outgoing and flirtatious, while Jennie tended to be more cautious. She didn't date much, not because she didn't get asked—this summer she'd met more guys than she had in her entire life. It was just that the guys she really liked were either too old—like Rocky—or weren't around—like Ryan.

"Wish me luck," Lisa yelled as she started to leave. "Oh, and call me if you hear anything about Gavin." She suddenly turned serious. "I wish there was more we could do."

"Me too. I might go out to his house after I talk to Lieutenant Rastovski. Thought I'd get a list of Gavin's friends—people he's talked to lately. Maybe his mom will let me look around his room."

"Um—do you want me to go with you, Jen?" Lisa chewed on her bottom lip. "I can watch Rafael and go to the mall anytime."

Jennie smiled. "No, but there is something you can do."

"What?"

"Remember yesterday at the Beaumonts when we were talking about Mrs. Mancini and Alex?"

"You want to meet them, right?"

"Uh-huh. I think it's time. Why don't you bring Alexis to the mall—I'll meet you there . . . say around one-thirty."

Half an hour later, Jennie parked her car, plugged the meter, and walked the two blocks to the police station. Lieutenant Rastovski was coming down the steps while she was still a block away. She hollered at him, but he either didn't hear her or didn't want to. He took off in the opposite direction. Not about to let him get away, Jennie broke into a run.

"Excuse me," she panted as she caught up to him at the intersection. "Lieutenant Rastovski? I left a message for you."

"I know. You had information about the Mancini case." Rastovski had one of those go-away-kid-you-bother-me looks.

Jennie ignored it. "See, I happen to know Mr. Mancini didn't write that suicide note."

"Is that right?"

The light changed and Jennie crossed the street with him. "Which means he was murdered."

Rastovski sighed. "Look, Miss McGrady. This is all very interesting, but I'm going to lunch now. If you want to talk to me, go back to the station and wait until I get back."

"But this is important."

"So's my stomach."

Jennie tagged after him, growling under her breath. She stopped at the next intersection when the light flashed *Don't Walk*. The lieutenant kept going. Jennie hurried after him and almost got hit by a driver making a right turn.

"You need to be more careful crossing the street," he muttered when she caught up to him again.

"Why can't you just take a minute and listen to me?"

He stopped. "All right. I'm listening."

"Mr. Mancini never would have called his daughter Alex. And the note wasn't on the computer screen when I was in the office."

He started walking again. "Suicide is still a possibility. The guy was using his position as a chemistry teacher to manufacture drugs. He steals the equipment, sets up shop, then his conscience starts bothering him. Crank tends to make people delusional and paranoid. We see a lot of violent acts."

Jennie heaved an exasperated sigh, continuing to tag along behind him, barely able to keep up with his long strides. How was she going to make him listen? She'd sensed from the beginning that Mr. Mancini had been murdered, and her hunches were usually right. Maybe if she told him that—*Yeah, right, McGrady. Tell him you have a gut feeling. He'll get a big laugh out of that.*

Lieutenant Rastovski stopped in front of Lacy's Deli. "It's been nice visiting with you, Miss McGrady, but this is where we part company."

"I can't believe you won't listen to me. All I'm asking is that we sit down together and go back over some of the evidence. If you found a suicide note on the computer, then someone put it there after I was in the office."

"Jennie—" If it was possible, he sounded even more irritated than he had before. "I know you want to help, but I can't discuss this case with you."

"I'm not asking you to discuss it. I want to tell you what

I saw and you can decide if there's a problem."

"Why is this so important to you?" He was melting.

"Because—if I'm right and Mr. Mancini really didn't commit suicide, you're letting someone get away with murder. And my friend Gavin Winslow may be the next victim."

He frowned. "Who's this Winslow character and what does he have to do with the case?"

Jennie started to tell him about Gavin, but the door to the deli opened and they had to move aside. Luscious smells wafted out and set Jennie's stomach to growling.

"Um . . . hold on." He glanced at the deli door that was slowly closing, then back at Jennie. "Tell you what. I'm starving and the smells coming out of this place are about to drive me nuts. Come on. I'll buy you lunch and you can tell me all about your friend and this murder theory of yours."

*Yes!* Jennie felt like punching the air and cheering. Instead, she thanked the lieutenant and walked inside when he opened the door. A waiter wearing a Jewish skull cap ushered them to the only empty booth. Jennie had the feeling her escort had been there many times before. She slid into the tan vinyl booth and tucked her bag against the wall.

"The usual, sir?" the waiter asked as he set a couple of beat-up and badly stained menus on the Formica table.

"Yep—and whatever the young lady wants."

Jennie glanced at the menu. "A roast turkey sandwich and a bottle of mineral water."

"You got it."

As soon as the waiter left, Jennie filled the lieutenant in on the conversation she'd had with Gavin the afternoon before he'd disappeared. "I can't believe you didn't know he was missing."

Rastovski scowled. "I can't either. If it's related to the Mancini case, someone should have told me. Though I'm not sure when they'd have had the time. So tell me more about

# JENNIE McGRADY MYSTERY

this kid. He was taking it upon himself to investigate Mancini's death?"

"He's a reporter and wanted me to help him. He called me around six last night and wanted to talk to me about a big breakthrough. I wasn't home so Mom took the message, only she didn't tell me until later. Anyway, he never went home last night."

"Here you go." The waiter set their orders down. "Condiments are behind you. Whistle if you need anything else."

Rastovski assured him they would. His "usual" turned out to be a bowl of soup and a six-inch-tall Reuben sandwich. By the time Jennie had pulled the fancy toothpicks out of her sandwich, Rastovski had downed half of his Reuben.

"Sorry to start ahead of you. I haven't had a chance to eat since two this morning."

"You were up all night?"

"Had three homicides last night." He stuffed a portion of sandwich in his mouth and wiped a drip of mustard off his chin.

Wow. No wonder he hadn't felt like talking about Mr. Mancini. Their conversation dwindled down to an occasional comment on the quality and portions of food while they finished eating. While Lieutenant Rastovski finished off his meal with coffee and a piece of deep-dish berry pie a la mode, Jennie dropped half of her meal into a doggy bag for Bernie.

She watched Rastovski eat for a moment. "If you ate like that in front of my mom, she'd have a fit."

"Why's that?"

"You're eating too fast."

"You're right. It comes with the job. Always eating on the run." He set his fork down and reached for his coffee. "I appreciate you telling me about your friend, but I wouldn't worry too much about him. He'll probably turn up in the next day or so. Every day we get dozens of calls from frantic

66

parents saying their teenager's missing. Some of them run away. Some get busy smoking joints and just don't bother to go home."

*Rastovski, you are a first-class jerk.* She wanted to say it— almost did, but she couldn't quite bring herself to it.

"Gavin isn't like that. He'd never—"

"Right. How many times have I heard that? Tell you what, Jennie. I should have reports from the crime lab and the medical examiner's office by now. I'll go over all the reports along with your statement. If you're right and we are dealing with a homicide—you'll be the first to know. But I wouldn't hold my breath if I were you. I don't think we're going to come up with anything other than suicide on this one."

# 8

On the way back to the station, Rastovski chewed on a toothpick and ignored Jennie for the first block. "Tell me something," he said when they stopped at an intersection. "I understand this isn't the first case you've shown an interest in. Officer Rockwell tells me you've developed quite a reputation for solving crimes. You just nosy, or what?"

Jennie glanced down at her scruffy tennis shoes, then met his gaze head on: "I'd like to go into law enforcement. My grandmother used to be a police officer here in Portland—and my father is—*was* a DEA agent." *Way to go, McGrady.* She hoped he hadn't noticed the slip.

"Yeah? Locally?"

"No, um—he was on a case when his plane went down in the Puget Sound area five years ago. They never found it."

"Must be tough."

Jennie shrugged. "Sometimes."

"You trying to fill his shoes? Happens sometimes. Kids lose a parent and kind of take over that parent's role."

"I'm not sure what you mean."

"Your father may have been a DEA agent, but you aren't. You need to stop trying to be your dad. Stop trying to prove Mancini was murdered."

He paused in front of the station. "I got enough to do without dealing with some kid who fancies herself another

68

Nancy Drew. I appreciate your concerns about whether or not this was a suicide, and I thank you for sharing your views. Now that you've done your duty, I want you to go home and forget about it. Go hang out with your friends or whatever kids your age do these days. And no more playing cops and robbers."

"But you said you were going to—"

"I will check into it, but you won't. Goodbye, Jennie. I'll be in touch."

*Jerk.* Jennie had a hard time understanding Rastovski's attitude. *I am not pretending to be my dad. I'm me.* Okay, so maybe this guy was overworked and had too many crimes to solve. That was no reason to treat her like she didn't have the intelligence God gave a goose.

At least she'd gotten him to agree to look over the evidence again. She'd liked to have followed the man into the station and told him off but remembered she'd parked in a half-hour zone over an hour ago. Jennie broke into a run and reached the ticketed car just as the meter maid, in her little white cart, putt-putted around the corner.

Rats. She kicked the Mustang's wheel. When the pain subsided, Jennie grabbed the ticket from under the windshield wiper, unlocked her car, and slid inside. "Why me?" she grumbled. "I should send the stupid ticket to Rastovski. It's his fault I'm late. If he'd—"

She threw the ticket on the seat, jammed the key in the ignition, and took a deep breath. She was not going to let him get to her. The lieutenant had suggested she go hang out with friends, and that's exactly what she planned to do.

———

Clackamas Town Center was packed with kids and parents taking advantage of the early back-to-school sales, and Jennie had to park in what felt like the next county. She wove through the crowds to the food court located just above the skating rink.

It took her fifteen minutes and two times around the court to spot Lisa, Allison, and B.J. Of course, part of that time had been spent on the phone to Mrs. Winslow. They still hadn't heard from Gavin.

"I wish there was something I could do," Jennie had told her.

"I know," Maddie said. "I appreciate that. Just keep praying. At least the police are more involved now. Your friend Rocky has been wonderful. He talked his superiors into launching a full investigation. We also got some news coverage, so we're hoping someone may have seen him."

Jennie hoped that was the case. *Keep praying*, Maddie had said. Jennie offered up a prayer as she made her way toward her friends.

"Hi!" Lisa waved her over. "We were about to give up on you."

Jennie folded herself into one of the four chairs attached to the table. "Sorry I'm late. It took me longer than I thought."

"Did you get to talk to the lieutenant?"

"Yeah, but he didn't seem too interested."

"What did he say?" Lisa stirred her drink with a straw.

Jennie outlined the main points. "Personally, I think he's more concerned about me minding my own business than learning the truth about Mr. Mancini."

"Well, you can't give up now. Alex should be here any minute. She had to go with her mom to make funeral arrangements."

"There they are." Allison stood up and waved to a tall, thin, dark-haired woman about Mom's age and a girl with short magenta-and-black-striped hair. They waved back. Mrs. Mancini opened her bag and extracted some money and handed it to Alex. The woman was wearing a pink linen-type suit and a matching hat and seemed out of place among the casually dressed shoppers, but then so did her daughter. Okay, so maybe Alex's appearance wasn't all that unusual. A lot of kids experimented with hair dyes and weird, off-the-wall clothes. But not at Trinity High. True, school hadn't started yet, but Alex Mancini had a lot of work to do if she planned to comply with the school's strict dress code.

Mrs. Mancini said something to Alex, then turned to go in the opposite direction. Jennie's gaze swung back to Alex. She was about Lisa's height, but weighed about twenty pounds more—of course some of that may have been the baggy overalls she was wearing. Her nearly white skin, blood red lipstick, and matching nail polish made her look like Dracula's sister.

"Excuse me while I go barf." B.J. picked up a tray and after depositing the garbage in the trash, set it on top of about a dozen other trays.

"B.J., be nice." Allison rolled her eyes and gave Jennie and Lisa a you'll-have-to-forgive-her-she's-nuts look.

"I am. It's the vampire you need to worry about." B.J. stopped behind Jennie and whispered, "Watch her fangs, McGrady. I'll call you later."

"Her what?" Jennie had heard her but was having a hard time understanding why B.J., of all people, was coming down so hard on the girl.

"Never mind. I'll let you figure it out for yourself."

"B.J., where will I find you?" Allison asked.

"Don't worry. I'll be back. Just don't leave without me."

"It would serve her right if I did." Allison sat back down. "It's nice having a sister at times, but she can be such a brat."

"Allison, Lisa, hi." Alex grinned, revealing a full set of braces. She plopped a huge canvas bag on B.J.'s chair, then reached inside to pull out a twenty. "I am so glad you called. Being around my family right now is not fun. They're constantly talking about death."

*Not unusual when someone has just died*, Jennie started to reply, but didn't.

"You must be Jennie. I have heard so much about you." She reached up and touched what looked like a diamond stud in her pierced left nostril. The red circle of skin around it made it look like a huge, glowing zit.

"I've heard a lot about you too." Jennie shifted her gaze from the nose to the eyes. Alex had turquoise eyes—the color of a chlorinated pool. Contacts, most likely. Jennie found it hard not to stare.

"Good stuff, I hope." Alex blinked and looked away.

You could tell a lot about people by their eyes. Alex was nervous about something—or afraid. Jennie had seen the look before in the eyes of a woman who was being abused by her husband. She couldn't help wondering about the girl in front of her.

"I—um—I'm sorry about your dad," Jennie said.

"Stepdad." She glanced at Allison and Lisa. "I'm starved. You guys want anything?"

Allison and Lisa both declined.

"A Diet Coke," Jennie said, digging into her wallet for money and pulling out a dollar bill and some change. "If you don't mind."

"Not at all." She waved Jennie's hand away. "My treat."

"Well," Jennie mused when she was out of earshot, "B.J. was right about one thing. She doesn't seem too broken up over her stepfather's death."

"I didn't know Mr. Mancini was her stepfather." Allison frowned. "Maybe she didn't like him."

Jennie stretched her long legs, leaned back, and folded her arms. "Did she ever talk about him?"

"I don't think so." Allison thought for a moment. "I did ask her once how it felt having a teacher for a parent. Can't remember what she said, but I don't think it was very complimentary."

"What are you thinking, Jennie?" Lisa placed her hand on Jennie's arm. "Oh, wait. You think he might have been abusing her?"

"The thought crossed my mind. Did she ever say anything—?"

"No." Both girls shook their heads.

Jennie had a lot of questions for Alex Mancini. Unfortunately, Lisa, Allison, and Alex went into a shopping mode and Jennie could do little more than tag along and pick up snatches of conversation.

"Oh, look, this will be perfect for your trip abroad." Allison held up a white and navy dress.

"What trip?" Jennie jerked to attention.

Alex draped the dress over her arm along with about five other outfits she'd picked out. "My mom and I are going to Europe."

"Really? Before school?"

"Yes, actually during school. We'll be living in England for six months."

"Wow. Sounds like fun."

"Oh, it will be, especially without—" Her lips clamped shut. "It's going to be a blast."

"Do you have relatives there or something?" Lisa asked.

"No. Mom says we'll stay in bed-and-breakfasts for a while, then she's going to try to find a place to rent."

"Sounds expensive." Jennie wandered to the next rack, pretending to be less interested than she really was.

"We can afford it. Tom left Mom and me a lot of money, and Mom has always wanted to go to Europe."

"So, when are you leaving?" Jennie picked a dress from the rack and held it up.

"In two weeks."

"You must have been planning this for a long time."

"Actually, no." Alex grabbed another dress and headed

73

for the dressing room. "Mom made the arrangements this morning."

"Did you hear that?" Jennie put the dress back and joined Lisa and Allison at a sales rack.

"You mean about the trip to Europe? Isn't that great?" Allison grinned. "We went last summer."

"I'd love to go to Europe," Lisa said. "Maybe Gram will take us sometime, Jennie. Wouldn't that be neat?"

"Don't you guys get it? That trip has got to cost a fortune."

"Well sure, but—"

"I could be wrong, but what kind of person would plan a six-month trip to Europe the same day she makes arrangements to bury her husband?"

Two hours and a dozen department stores later, Jennie dropped into one of the chairs in the shoe department in Nordstrom. After sitting for a few more minutes, watching Lisa and Allison give their opinion while Alex tried on shoes, Jennie announced she was leaving.

"Oh no, Jennie." Lisa sidestepped half a dozen boxes and crossed the aisle to where Jennie was sitting. "You can't go yet—we haven't done any shopping for you."

Jennie shook her head. "Not today. You know how I feel about shopping. It's fun for a while, but I'm bored out of my skull." She lowered her voice. "Besides, the main reason I came was to talk to Alex, and I think I've gotten about all I'm going to."

Lisa sighed. "Okay. Are you going out to Gavin's?"

"I don't think so. I'll probably call before I leave here, though."

"I sure hope he's turned up."

"Me too." Jennie backed away. "Call me later. Oh, and try to find out what Mr. Mancini was like at home."

After taking the escalator upstairs, Jennie made her way back to customer service and plugged a quarter in the pay phone. Mrs. Winslow picked up on the third ring.

"It's me, Jennie. Any word on Gavin?"

"No, but I'm glad you called. There was an inspector here looking for you—Ratski or something like that."

"Rastovski?"

"Right. He was here with a DEA agent and said he needed to ask you some questions. Apparently Michael told them you might be here. He wanted me to have you call him."

Jennie thanked her and hung up. DEA? Her heart did a triple flip. For a moment she let herself fantasize that the agent was her father, but only for a moment. *Forget it, McGrady. It isn't going to happen.*

# 9

Jennie retrieved Lieutenant Rastovski's card and plunked another quarter into the pay phone. He wasn't in. "No, he can't call me back. Just tell him I'll be home in twenty minutes. I'll try again from there."

Rastovski and the DEA agent were waiting in her driveway when she got home. He wasn't her father—at least she didn't think so. This guy had more hair—a sandy gray color. He looked like any other guy, really. A brown tweed sports jacket and tan slacks. He was leaning against a deep green Honda Accord. An unmarked police car, she realized as she pulled up beside it. He had an unlit cigarette dangling from his mouth that he tucked into his shirt pocket.

"Jennie," Rastovski greeted when she stepped out of her Mustang. "This is an old friend of mine with the DEA, Steve Douglas."

"Hi, Jennie." He reached out a hand and Jennie shook it. His blue gaze met hers head on. "The lieutenant's been telling me about the Mancini case and your interest in it."

They were definitely not Dad's eyes. Jennie let her gaze travel back to Rastovski.

He answered her question before she could ask it. "The DEA has an interest in the case, and Steve here wants to ask you a few questions. After reading over the reports on Mancini's death, I have a couple more questions of my own."

They were taking her seriously. She couldn't believe it. "Sure. Um—do you want to come inside?"

"Actually, we'd like you to come to the high school," Rastovski said. "Show us exactly what you did and saw."

"This may sound stupid, but why didn't you have me do that before?"

"Mr. Rhodes thought it would be too traumatic for you."

"Michael should mind his own business," Jennie muttered. "I could have handled it."

The two men looked at each other, then back at Jennie.

Okay, so maybe seeing a dead body would have given her nightmares for the next ten years, she admitted to herself. Maybe Michael had been right, but he shouldn't have made the decision for her. He was not her father. Changing the subject she asked, "Do you want me to drive my car or come with you?"

"You'd better meet us out there." Douglas's keys jangled as he pulled them out of his pocket.

Jennie nodded. "I need to leave Mom a note." She glanced at her watch. Nearly five. Mom and Nick would be home soon. "I'll meet you there in about half an hour—unless the traffic is really bad. Um, Lieutenant Rastovski," she called him back, "does this mean you've decided to call Mancini's death a homicide?"

"Beginning to look that way."

Jennie could feel the makings of a smile curl her lips. She loved being right.

When the men left, Jennie let herself into the house. A note tacked on the refrigerator told her Mom had already been there and gone. *Having dinner at Kevin and Kate's tonight with Gram and J.B. See you there. Love, Mom.*

Jennie called Aunt Kate's. Gram answered.

"Sweetheart, I'm so glad you called. You will be here tonight, won't you? I've missed you terribly."

"I've missed you too." It felt good hearing Gram's voice

again. "I'll be there, but I have to meet Lieutenant Rastovski and a DEA agent out at Trinity High so I might be late. What time's dinner?"

"Probably around seven. We'll wait for you."

"Did you hear about Mr. Mancini?"

"I've been reading about it in the papers, and your mother's been filling us in on the details. I'm sorry you had to be there when it happened."

"Actually, I'm glad I was there. Otherwise the police might have dismissed it as a suicide."

"You don't think it was?"

"No, but I'll talk to you about that later. I gotta run."

Traffic wasn't bad until she reached Highway 26. Her half-hour guess had been a good one. In exactly thirty-two minutes she pulled into the Trinity parking lot. There were two cars already parked in the main lot in front of the complex—Michael's BMW and Douglas's Honda. Both were empty.

Jennie took a deep breath to settle the butterflies in her stomach. She didn't know why she felt nervous. She just did. The butterflies were still dive-bombing when Jennie walked down the hall with Rastovski and Douglas. They'd wanted to question her and Michael separately.

"Okay." Jennie paused at the door to the chemistry lab. Her face was hot and sweaty enough to dampen her bangs. "It was about one o'clock when I opened the door. I went in. The first thing I noticed was the dark—and this antiseptic smell—like someone had just cleaned it. I smelled something else too—like sulphur. I didn't think much of it at first, because chemistry labs usually smell strange. I figured Mr. Mancini had been experimenting. It wasn't until I found out that Mr. Mancini had been shot that I realized the sulphur smell might have been from the gun."

Douglas raised an eyebrow. "And that's a scent you're familiar with?"

"My grandmother's taken me to the shooting range where she practices a few times. It's been a while, but—" Jennie shrugged.

"Her grandmother is an ex-cop," Rastovski supplied the explanation as he glanced around the room. "Jennie, I'd like you to retrace your steps for us."

She nodded. "I set my bag down and turned on the light. That's when I noticed the counters were damp—like they'd just been cleaned. Oh—" She glanced up toward the row of windows. They were all closed. "One of those windows was open—the second one over."

Rastovski and Douglas both paused to look up, then jotted the information down on their pads.

"This open window," Douglas mused. "Was it finger-printed?"

"Yep," Rastovski said. "Only prints we found were the janitor's and Mancini's."

"As I recall, the window had been open after the burglary as well, right?" Douglas walked to the window to examine it more closely.

"That's right, but I don't think the killer came in and out that way. There were pry marks around the window, but no scuff marks on the sill or wall to indicate that anyone had climbed in or out. I have a hunch the window was left open to lead us to believe someone had broken in."

"Hmm." Douglas frowned as he ran his hand along the wall. Both men went back to where Jennie was standing, and Rastovski asked her to continue.

"I called to Mr. Mancini. He didn't answer, but I heard a sound in the office and went to look."

Jennie led them into the room and explained about the open door and the papers on the floor.

"What did you do with the papers?" Rastovski frowned.

"I picked the ones up that were on the floor and set them on top of the desk."

"Are you sure?"

"Yeah, why?"

"The desk was like this when I got here. Neat and tidy."

"Someone cleaned it up after I left then." Jennie stepped around the desk. The computer displayed the same screen saver she'd seen before. "The newspaper said the suicide note was on the screen, but that's not what I saw."

"So you say. According to Phelps, you thought it was a formula or equation of some sort." Standing beside her, Rastovski tapped the space bar. "The suicide note is still here. This is what was on the computer when we got here. The attending officer's report confirms it."

"Can you remember anything about the formula you saw, Jennie?" Douglas came up behind her and looked at the screen.

"Not really. I mean, I wasn't paying that much attention. If I'd known about"—her gaze darted into the other room—"about Mr. Mancini. If I'd known it was evidence I'd have written it down. I might be able to remember parts of it." Jennie picked up a piece of scratch paper from beside the phone and began drawing figures as she remembered them.

Douglas eased in front of her and pulled out the chair, then sat down. "Let's see what kind of files your teacher had on this thing. Maybe I can find something that looks like what you saw."

For the next few minutes the DEA agent's fingers clicked across the keyboard. Jennie paused in her drawing to watch as he called up a number of documents under the heading "corres," like Trinity, general, Dawson, and several others Jennie didn't recognize. Under Trinity there were several files named Michael—then a number and a letter. The same for Pastor Dave and another grouping for the school's principal. Easy enough to figure out.

Douglas called up the latest memo to Michael, dated the day before Mr. Mancini's death. Looking over Douglas's shoulder, Jennie scanned the text. It was short and to the point.

*I understand your desire to assist the young man we spoke about yesterday. After going over his files, however, I've decided to deny your request. Sincerely, Tom Mancini*

Jennie wondered who the young man was and why Mancini hadn't mentioned a name.

Douglas zipped through several other files and menus. All easily assessable. Except the one named Dawson. "Looks like he didn't want anyone to see it—which means we'll have to find a way to access it. I want to know what's in there."

Rastovski rubbed a hand across his chin and gave Jennie a cursory glance. "I appreciate your help on this, Jennie. You can go on home now. We'll take it from here."

Jennie's stomach contracted. She hated being dismissed like that. Still, she supposed she should go. Kate was waiting dinner for her. While she watched the two investigators, an idea took form.

She cleared her throat and swallowed the grapefruit-sized lump in her throat. "I—I think I know of a way to catch the killer."

Douglas whirled around in the chair and Rastovski turned and looked at her as if she'd grown two heads.

They didn't ask, but she told them anyway. "I must have scared away Mr. Mancini's killer. It would have been easy for him—or her—to hide close by. The woods are only a few feet away. Anyway, when I left, they must have come back inside, straightened Mr. Mancini's desk, and written the note. The point is, whoever killed him knows I was there. I even said my name. Since you've been calling it a suicide, the killer has nothing to worry about. But now that we know it was a murder—I mean, I really don't know much, but what if we tell the press I saw the person running away and could make a positive identification."

"No." Rastovski's dark eyebrows almost met when he

frowned. "It's too dangerous."

"He's right, Jennie." Douglas swung back around to the computer. "Better leave this to the police."

"You could wire me and have someone watching."

Neither man answered. "Wait a second." Rastovski pointed to the screen. "Looks like Mancini's lab assistant has logged in a lot of hours this summer."

"You talk to him?" Douglas asked

"Not yet." Rastovski eyed the screen, then jotted something down in his notebook. Jennie eased up behind them and read the name on the screen. Curtis Bolton.

"Gavin knew about him," Jennie murmured, remembering the name Gavin had written in his notebook just before he closed it.

"The kid who's missing?" Douglas asked. "How well do you know this Curtis guy?"

"Not well. I remember seeing him around, but we never really talked. He's a senior. Quiet. Studious."

"Any friends?"

Jennie shook her head. "I don't know. I never saw him hanging out with anyone from school. And he didn't come to our youth group at church."

Douglas thanked her and stayed with the computer. Rastovski walked her back through the lab. "Appreciate your help, Jennie. We may need to talk to you again, but you can go on home now."

She was being dismissed again. Maybe they figured it was the only way to get rid of her. Jennie wanted to hang out with them—learn as much as she could. "Don't know why they couldn't have taken my suggestion," she muttered. "I don't mind being bait."

"Going fishing?" Michael asked.

She jumped. "What—?" Jennie had been looking at the mottled shadows on the floor and hadn't seen him approach.

"You said something about bait."

"Oh. No. Um—just talking to myself. You going down to talk to Rastovski and Douglas?"

"Yes. Though I don't know what more I can tell them. I'll be glad when this is over."

"Michael, there was a letter on Mr. Mancini's computer about a student you and he were talking about. He decided not to honor your request."

Michael shook his head. "I'm afraid that's privileged information, Jennie."

She glanced back at the lab. "They're going to ask you about it."

"They'll get the same answer I've given you."

"Can't you tell me anything? Not even what it was about?"

He shrugged. "This was all being handled in confidence. Just someone who wanted another chance. Mancini was being a—never mind. I'd better get going."

"Are you coming to dinner tonight at Aunt Kate's?"

"No. I have some paper work I have to catch up on. Say hello to everyone for me."

"Sure." She went a few feet, then stopped and spun around. "Michael?"

He paused and turned, hands in his pockets.

"What's going on with Gavin? Any word?"

"I wish I knew. He seems to have vanished."

She wanted to ask him more, but this wasn't the time. Later, maybe tomorrow, she'd ask him about Curtis. Or more to the point, how well did Gavin know Curtis? Could the lab assistant be mixed up in this? And where was he?

Jennie watched Michael until he entered the lab, then jogged past the office and out the main entrance, pawing through her bag for her keys as she went. When she got home she'd draw a chart and plug in names of possible suspects like she'd done on other cases. She stopped herself in mid-thought. *What are you doing, McGrady? Now that the police know it's a murder they'll handle it.*

Jennie looked at her reflection in the car window. She knew herself pretty well, and the face looking back at her was one of determination. She hadn't meant to get involved. Probably should just let it go. But she was in too deep and knew she wouldn't be able to rest until Mancini's killer had been brought to justice.

Jennie stuck her key in the lock, then realized she'd forgotten to lock it. She slid onto the seat and checked the rear-view mirror. Just as the engine roared to life, she heard a noise behing her.

Jennie's heart leapt into her throat. She gripped the steering wheel. *You should have checked, McGrady. Always look in and around the car before you get in.* Too late she remembered number three in the list of safety rules Gram had given her. The hairs on her neck stood erect.

She heard the sound again.

Someone was in the backseat.

# 10

Jennie squeezed her eyes closed, half expecting to feel a gun at the back of her head—or a knife at her throat.

Little by little the panic subsided. Nothing happened. Had she imagined the sounds? No, there it was again. Jennie glanced in the rearview mirror. No sinister face looked back. Taking a deep breath, she ventured a look into the backseat.

"Gavin!"

Jennie's screech brought a grimace to his haggard features. He covered his eyes and moved his lips, but nothing came out. He looked rumpled and confused.

"What are you doing here? Where have you been?" The questions poured out of Jennie's mouth, but she may as well have been talking to a mannequin. Adrenalin still pumping through her veins, she shot out of the car and pushed the seat forward.

"Gavin, for Pete's sake, what's going on? Are you hurt?"

He groaned and peered at her through glazed eyes.

Other than several facial bruises and some scratches on his arm, Jennie couldn't see any injuries, but she wasn't about to take a chance on moving him.

"Stay here. I'm going for help."

"No," he gasped. "Wait." He reached out a hand to stop her, but it fell back against his chest.

"I'll be right back. The police are in the chemistry lab with Michael. They'll help."

Ignoring his protests, Jennie raced into the building and down the hall. Her shouts brought Michael, Rastovski, and Douglas running.

"It's Gavin. He's in the backseat of my car. I was afraid to move him. He might be hurt. I can't be sure, but from the way he was acting, I think he may have been drugged."

The two officers charged ahead. By the time Michael and Jennie joined them, which couldn't have been more than a few seconds, Douglas was on the radio.

"What is this, a joke?" Rastovski had his hand on top of the Mustang's open door.

"What do you mean?" Jennie approached the car. The backseat was empty. "He was here. I swear."

"You're sure?"

"Of course. Not even my imagination could come up with something like that. He can't have gotten far. He looked really sick. We have to find him."

"All right, I'll take your word for it."

Douglas called for backup. Rastovski shouted orders. "Rhodes, check inside the school. Steve and I will head into the woods."

"What about me?" Jennie pushed in front of Michael.

"Stay here." Rastovski raked his fingers through his hair.

"But—"

"In case he comes back."

"Do it, Jennie," Michael warned, then ran back inside the building.

Jennie was tempted to ignore their orders but instead slammed the car door shut and leaned against it. "What is going on here, Gavin?" she muttered.

Gavin must have crawled into her car, but where had he been all this time? Had someone kidnapped him and drugged him, then let him go? But why? What had he stumbled into?

Jennie shoved the questions aside. Gavin had a lot of explaining to do when—if—they were able to find him again.

They would, she was certain of that. Like she'd told the lieutenant, Gavin couldn't have gone far. Unless he'd been faking. Jennie doubted that. In his condition, Gavin would barely have been able to get out of the car, let alone run away.

*Wait a minute, McGrady. Maybe he didn't even try to run. Maybe he's closer than anyone imagined.* Jennie pushed away from the car and walked toward the school.

The landscaping on either side of the entrance consisted of a dozen or so rhododendrons of various sizes pressed against the brick facing. In front of them was about a three-foot band of azaleas. Then came the lower shrubs and flowering plants. Jennie stepped over the curb and crossed the narrow expanse of lawn to the flower garden to the left side of the steps, nearest her car.

There were no clear footprints. A thick layer of bark dust covered the ground. Jennie hunkered down to examine the area more closely. Most of the bark had faded, but beside a clump of purple-blue lobelia, Jennie spotted a small patch of darker wood chips that had been turned over. As if someone had stepped wrong and churned it up. A short distance beyond that was another.

Jennie inched deeper into the plants, taking care not to step on them. When she reached the large rhodies in the back, she paused, then eased the branches aside.

"Don't come any closer or I'll shoot." Gavin's voice was hoarse. He sat cross-legged on the ground leaning against the building. His matted hair stood up at odd angles.

Jennie scrunched down and crawled toward him, pushing his weapon—a foot-long stick—to the side. "Put that thing away before you poke someone's eyes out."

"I mean it, get away from me." Staring wild-eyed, he jabbed it at her.

She jumped back. "What is *wrong* with you?"

"Leave me alone. Got to find—my—my . . ." He looked like he was about to cry.

"Gavin, put that thing down and let me help you."

"No—I can't. Go away before I shoot—"

She didn't hear the rest. Someone grabbed her around the waist and yanked her backward.

"What do you think you're doing?" she screamed at Rastovski.

The lieutenant didn't stop until they reached the Mustang. "Stay down," he growled, his arm pinning her in place.

The next few seconds cut into slow motion, and Jennie felt like she'd been thrown on to a television production of *Homicide*.

"Police! Come out with your hands above your head. Now!" Douglas crouched beside the stairs, about twenty feet away, his gun trained at the big rhododendron that still hid Gavin. Michael hunkered down behind him.

Lieutenant Rastovski moved away from her. Using the car as a shield, he drew his weapon.

"Don't shoot him!" Jennie grabbed at Rastovski's jacket and pulled him back.

The bushes parted. Gavin came out, but his hands weren't up. He yelled something Jennie couldn't understand and charged straight at Douglas.

"No!" Michael slammed his fist down on Douglas's arm just as the agent fired.

It seemed forever before anyone spoke. Douglas called for an ambulance.

Stunned, Jennie stared at Gavin writhing on the grass, turning patches of it crimson with blood. She broke away from Rastovski and ran to help her friend. Blood pumped out of a gaping wound in his thigh, saturating his jeans.

*Stop the bleeding.* She could almost hear her CPR instructor's voice going back over the procedures. Mechanically, Jennie pressed her hand against the wound, pinning his leg to the ground.

"Don't touch me!" Gavin struggled against her.

"Hold still," she yelled when he tried to kick her away.

Rastovski knelt beside her and opened up a first-aid kit he'd gotten from Douglas's trunk. "The way that sucker is pumping, I must have hit an artery." Douglas came up on the other side. He and Michael held Gavin down. Rastovski and Jennie applied a tourniquet and wrapped the wound.

A fire truck barreled in a few minutes later. Two EMTs jumped out, grabbed their supplies, and jogged toward them.

Ten minutes later Jennie's hands shook as she pressed the soap dispenser in the girls' rest room and washed Gavin's blood from her hands and arms. She couldn't be sure what shook her up the most—the shooting or Rastovski's rage.

The moment the ambulance left, he turned on her. "Don't you ever do anything like that again."

The lieutenant didn't have to explain what she'd done wrong. Jennie knew. She and Michael could both face charges for interfering with an officer. "He didn't have a gun," Jennie had argued. "You might have killed him."

"What if he'd *had* a gun, Jennie? What if he'd come out of those bushes waving an automatic rifle? We'd all be dead."

"But he didn't. You shouldn't have gone after him like that. I was doing just fine."

"He was threatening you."

"With a stick. I don't think he even knew what he was saying. You sound like you're sorry he wasn't hurt worse—or killed."

Rastovski drew a hand down his face, over his mustache, and was probably counting to ten. "Look, we'll talk about this later. I want you down at the station tomorrow morning." He looked over at Michael. "That goes for you too."

Douglas and Rastovski left a few minutes later to follow up with Gavin. Michael had sent her into the rest room to clean up with the promise he'd be waiting for her when she finished.

Jennie caught sight of her reflection in the mirror. A rust

streak ran across one cheek where she'd used her blood-streaked hand to brush the tears from her face. She hadn't meant to cry. It shouldn't have mattered what Rastovski and Douglas thought of her. But it did. In their minds, she'd messed up royally.

*You did the right thing*, she reminded herself. *So did Michael. If you hadn't intervened, Gavin might be dead.*

"You okay?" Michael asked when she got back to the office.

She nodded. "I guess." She glanced at her watch. Five after seven. "Looks like I'm late again. I'd better call and tell them I won't be there for dinner."

"I'm sure they'll wait for you, Jennie." He squeezed her shoulder.

"I know that. It's just—I have to go to the hospital. Make sure Gavin's okay."

"Let me do that. From the condition he was in, I don't think he'll be able to have visitors for some time."

"But I need to find out what happened to him. It's obvious he was high on something."

"Hmm. Sad, isn't it? You think you know someone and—"

"You don't think Gavin took drugs on his own, do you?"

"Do you have a better explanation?"

"Yeah, I do. Somebody killed Mr. Mancini. Gavin knew that, and I think he may have been getting too close. Maybe the killer abducted Gavin and drugged him to get him out of the way."

"That doesn't make sense, Jennie. Why wouldn't Mancini's murderer just kill Gavin as well?"

"Maybe he was going to—and Gavin escaped." Jennie tucked an annoying strand of hair behind an ear.

"There's really no point second guessing, is there? Hopefully tomorrow he'll be able to tell us what this disappearance thing was all about."

Jennie didn't know if she could wait that long. Okay, so she'd have dinner with her family. *Then* she'd drive to the hospital.

Before leaving the school, Jennie called Aunt Kate to explain what had happened. "I'll be there in about ten minutes."

"No problem. I'll put the spaghetti on."

Despite all that had happened, Jennie's stomach warmed at the thought of eating Aunt Kate's spaghetti. The rich meat sauce would have simmered all day in her industrial-sized crock pot. They'd have salad and warm, toasty garlic bread.

When Jennie pulled up to the curb, Bernie, Nick, Lisa, and Kurt, Lisa's little brother, ran out to meet her.

"'Bout time you got here. We're starving." Kurt's freckled cheeks were flushed and hot. His chestnut curls hung limp on his brow.

"Sorry about that, but I had an emergency." Jennie stroked Bernie's silky fur.

He welcomed her with a bark and a slurpy kiss on her hand.

"How come you've got blood all over you?" Lisa asked.

"Oh, gross." Jennie glanced down at the rust-colored splatters on her lavender knit shirt and blue jeans. "I should have gone home to change."

"Don't worry about it. You can wear something of mine," Lisa said.

Nick wrapped his skinny arms around his sister's leg and hung there while she started up the driveway. "Where was you?"

"Where *were* you?" Jennie corrected.

Nick giggled. "I been here. Where was you?"

She rumpled his hair and pulled him up into her arms. "Oh, man, you are getting to be one heavy dude."

"I'm forty-one pounds."

"Mom said you found Gavin." Lisa came up beside her.

"Yep." Jennie gave her an I'll-tell-you-later look.

"Did the police believe you about the m-u-r-d-e-r?" She spelled out the last word.

"Uh-huh. At least I think so." She deposited Nick on the steps.

He shot into the house behind Kurt, yelling, "She's here! She's here. Now can we eat?"

"It's almost ready," Aunt Kate hollered back.

"We've still got a few minutes before dinner. Let's go up to my room so you can change. Mom," Lisa called, "we'll be in my room. Call us when dinner's ready."

"Will do. Hi, Jennie."

"Hi!" Through the sliding glass doors that led out onto the patio, Jennie could see Mom, Gram, J.B., and Uncle Kevin talking. They looked up when they heard Lisa and waved. Jennie waved back, then dutifully followed her cousin to her bedroom.

Lisa pulled a denim skirt and sleeveless blouse out of her closet and tossed them at Jennie. "These should fit you—they're a little too big for me right now."

"Wish I had time for a shower," Jennie shrugged out of her blood-stained shirt and slipped on the fresh one. She snagged a brush from the dresser, plopped onto Lisa's bed, and began loosening her braid.

"Hand me the brush. Let me do it. You talk." Lisa climbed onto the bed behind Jennie.

"What did your Mom tell you?"

"Just that you found Gavin and he's in the hospital. I have a feeling she left out a lot."

"She did." Jennie leaned back as Lisa brushed through her hair. "You should have seen him. I don't know what he was on, but it made him crazy. He threatened to kill me with a stick." Jennie gave Lisa the highlights.

Lisa remained silent as Jennie spoke. And no wonder. As

the scene replayed itself in Jennie's head, it seemed unreal—
like it hadn't really happened.

Lisa finished Jennie's braid and gave it a tug. "All done."

After setting the brush on the dresser, Lisa settled back
on the bed. "How could they have shot him, Jennie? I mean,
he didn't have a gun—and how much harm could he do with
a stick?"

"It was a mistake. Rastovski and Douglas heard him
threaten me. They couldn't see him and thought he was
armed. They were trying to protect me."

"Poor Gavin. I'd like to go with you to the hospital after
dinner."

"Sure."

"Um—" Lisa glanced down at her hands and splayed her
fingers. She'd painted the nails a pale pink to match the
shorts outfit she wore. "I found out something today—about
Alex."

"Yeah?"

"First, she hated her stepfather. When I asked if he
abused her, she said not in the way I was thinking. The main
reason Alex was mad at him was because of the way he'd
treated her boyfriend."

"Girls!" Aunt Kate knocked on the door. "Dinner's on.
We're eating on the patio. Just dish up your plates and join
us."

"Be right there," Lisa answered, then turned back to Jennie.

"Who's her boyfriend?"

"Brian Stone."

"You're kidding." Somehow Jennie had trouble picturing
the eccentric Alexis Mancini with the tall, blond jock. Brian
was a total sports nut. He'd asked Jennie out a couple of
times, but she'd refused. Not that he wasn't cute. The guy
looked like a blond Tom Cruise. He just happened to be a
few sandwiches short of a picnic in the brains department.

"No, I'm not, but get this. Mancini flunked Brian last year. Brian tried to get reinstated and said he'd do a summer class. Mancini wouldn't take him back."

"Which means no football this fall." Jennie followed Lisa into the kitchen and grabbed a plate. Jennie wondered if Brian had been the student Mancini had written to Michael about.

"Exactly. The thing is, with Mancini out of the way, Brian gets another chance."

"So you're thinking he might have killed Mancini?" She piled spaghetti on her plate and stirred the thick, savory meat sauce.

"Or maybe Alex and Brian did it together."

# 11

"I hope you don't mind my accompanying you to visit your friend. Lisa seemed rather relieved when I offered to go in her place." Gram slid in behind the wheel of her cherry red 1955 classic Thunderbird convertible.

"Not at all. I love being with you—and riding in your car."

Lisa had begged off after getting a phone call from Rafael and inviting him over. The way she'd bounced around, you'd have thought she'd been nominated for an Academy Award. Jennie didn't think any guy was worth that much excitement. Except maybe Ryan. She was getting butterflies just thinking about his finally coming home.

"Good. I've been wanting to talk with you." Gram started the engine and adjusted the rearview mirror.

"Me too—I mean, to talk to you." Jennie buckled her seat belt—Gram had had them installed in the antique car several years ago when Oregon passed a mandatory seat belt law. Other than the belts, and an occasional part, Gram tried to stay true to the car's original design.

"Um—did Mom say anything about my coming down to the beach and staying with you for a week or two before school starts?"

"As a matter a fact, she did." Looking behind her, Gram backed out of the driveway and onto the street.

"And?"

"I think it's a wonderful idea. So does J.B. Do you want to come with us tomorrow?"

"Um—no—I mean, I'd like to, but I can't leave right now."

Gram smiled in understanding. "Of course, your friend Gavin."

"I wouldn't feel right about leaving until I know if he's going to be all right."

"Have you any ideas regarding the Mancini case? I've been following the story in the news. Do the police still think he committed suicide? He didn't, you know."

"I know—I spent half the day trying to tell Lieutenant Rastovski that. But how did you know? Did Lisa tell you?"

"We talked about it. But I'd already questioned the idea from what I'd gleaned from the papers and television."

"Why?"

"I found it rather odd that a man who took such pride in his work and who had just cleaned his own chemistry lab would then mess it up by shooting himself."

"That's exactly what Gavin told me." Jennie tipped her head back and smiled. She didn't know what felt best—knowing Gram shared her views, or feeling the warm summer wind whipping around her as she snuggled against the leather seats. "What does J.B. think about it?"

"The case is out of his jurisdiction, of course, but he agrees. Now tell me how you managed to get involved in all of this."

Jennie spent most of the drive to the hospital filling Gram in on the events of the past two days.

"A baffling case," Gram said, turning into the hospital parking lot. "Even more baffling is the man himself."

"What do you mean?"

"I did some checking of my own, and it seems your Mr. Mancini has a rather interesting past—some of which may

96

have swayed Lieutenant Rastovski to so stubbornly hold on to the idea of suicide."

"Really?" Jennie smoothed back the hair that had escaped her braid to ride the wind.

Gram finger-combed her own windblown salt-and-pepper hair. Like magic, it settled into place. "Come on," she said, opening the car door. "I'll tell you on the way in."

When Jennie joined her behind the car, Gram gave her a one-armed hug. "Have I told you lately how proud I am of you?"

"Yeah, but you can tell me again." Changing the subject, Jennie said, "By the way, I like your new haircut."

They began walking toward the hospital's main entrance. "So do I. It is so much easier to take care of than the shoulder-length style I'd been wearing."

"Gram?"

"Yes, darling?"

"You were going to tell me about Mr. Mancini."

"Yes, I guess I was." She frowned. "Jennie, by telling you this, I don't mean to encourage you to carry out your own investigation in this case. In fact, I've been commissioned by your mother to find out exactly what it is you're up to and put a stop to it."

Jennie chewed her lower lip and after a few seconds said, "I'm not investigating—I mean—not really."

Gram gave her a skeptical look.

"I'm just asking a few questions. You know how I am. I don't mean to go against Mom. But, Gram, telling me to stop thinking about it is like telling me not to breathe."

"Which is what makes it so hard for me to have to discourage you. You are far too much like me in that regard. But we are dealing with a murder here. It's one thing for you to speculate about it with me, but quite another to get physically involved."

"I've already had enough lectures from Rocky and Lieutenant Rastovski. All I can promise is that if I find out anything relating to the case, I'll tell the police."

Gram nodded. "I guess that will have to do." The automatic doors swished open as they approached.

"I don't understand why everybody has to be so paranoid. I've solved seven cases in the last three months. Not by myself, of course, but I helped."

"Yes, and unfortunately you've given all of us cause for concern. Jennie, if your mother seems overprotective at times it's because she loves you. She doesn't want to see you get hurt—none of us do."

"I won't get hurt."

"My dear girl, may I remind you that this summer alone you've been kidnapped, held at gunpoint, narrowly escaped a fire, been shot at, and had your arm broken."

"It was just a small break." Jennie held up her right arm. "See, they even took the cast off early."

"I know you plan on going into law enforcement, and I think that's wonderful. But don't ever minimize the danger."

Jennie didn't want to argue with Gram—or anybody for that matter. She didn't mean to be disagreeable, but why couldn't they understand? "Nancy Drew never had problems like this," Jennie muttered. "People practically knocked her door down trying to get her to investigate crimes."

Gram smiled. "Nancy Drew is a fictional character. You are real and very much alive, and we'd like to keep you that way."

Despite her annoyance, Jennie chuckled. "Okay, just tell Mom I won't do anything you wouldn't do."

"Oh, that's very funny. I'm sure that will make her feel much better."

"Well, it should. Especially since she doesn't know about your undercover work."

"Shh. You're not supposed to know either."

They stopped at the front desk and got Gavin's room number.

"We'd better table this discussion for now." Gram led the way down the hall and into the gift shop. "Would you like to pick up a gift for Gavin? Flowers? Balloons?"

After making a mental note to remind Gram to tell her what she'd learned about Mr. Mancini, Jennie said, "Balloons."

They bought one nylon balloon with a duck on it proclaiming, "Get well soon" and two bright blue latex balloons to accompany it. After picking out a get-well card and signing it, they headed for the elevator.

Gavin was lying in a bed rigged with some kind of traction device. His right leg had been raised off the bed and rested in a sling. A trapeze-like bar hung over his head. He reached to grab it when he saw her, his face contorting with pain.

Maddie Winslow was sitting beside the bed, typing on a laptop computer—probably working on her latest book. She wrote mysteries for young adults and was hoping to break into movies with one of the cases Jennie had helped solve this summer.

"Hi." Jennie stepped into the room, careful not to snag the balloons in the doorway.

"Jennie." Maddie looked up from her screen. "Your mother said you'd be by." Her gaze drifted to Gram. "Helen, how nice to see you again."

Gram returned the greeting and asked Gavin how he was doing.

"Wonderful." He sounded hoarse. "I've always wanted to know what it felt like to get shot—now I know."

"At least you haven't lost your sense of humor."

"Nope, only blood." He licked his lips. Maddie picked up a glass of water and placed the straw in his mouth. After a couple of swallows he pushed it away.

"They're giving him two units of packed cells," Maddie

said, nodding toward the IV stand and bags hanging there. One was blood, the other some sort of saline solution. "The bullet fractured his femur."

The strange effects of whatever drug or drugs he'd been on seemed to be gone. His eyes no longer had that wild look. He just looked like any normal person would in his condition.

"Um—" Jennie held the balloon bouquet toward him. "These are for you."

"Thanks."

"They're lovely." Maddie took them and secured the strings to Gavin's tray table.

Jennie opened her mouth to ask Gavin where he had disappeared to and how he'd ended up in her car, but he'd closed his eyes. She asked his mom instead. Maddie motioned them outside the room and closed the door. "We should let him rest."

"I'm sorry. I guess I shouldn't be asking questions."

"It's all right, Jennie. The police told us what happened and—I'm just so grateful you and Michael were there."

"Did you find out what kind of drug he was on?"

She shook her head. "The doctor said it may have been a methamphetamine, or possibly LSD, but we don't know yet."

"Gavin didn't say?"

"Gavin says he can't remember anything. The police tried to question him but finally gave up. I guess we'll have to wait until tomorrow. Maybe he'll be more coherent. I certainly hope so." Maddie started to cry.

Gram placed an arm around Maddie's shoulders in an effort to comfort her.

"What are we going to do? Gavin's never done anything like this before. He's always been so dependable."

"You don't think he took drugs himself, do you?" Jennie asked.

Maddie shook her head and blew her nose with the tissue

Gram handed her. "No, of course not. It's just that the police keep telling me he did. When I stand up for Gavin, they act like I'm lying."

They talked a few minutes longer, then at nine-fifteen Jennie and Gram left.

"I hate this." Jennie followed Gram into the elevator and hit the button for the first floor.

"What's that, dear?"

"Not knowing what's going on with Gavin. I wish I could say for sure he wasn't taking drugs. Thing is, I don't know him well enough to say that."

"Hmm. What do your instincts tell you?"

The elevator doors opened and they stepped out. Jennie thought for a moment before she answered. Instincts. Gram had always told her to trust them—that often it was the Holy Spirit whispering truth. "I guess if I had to choose based on what I know about Gavin, I'd side with Maddie. I don't think Gavin took the drugs on his own."

"Then that's what you need to hold on to. Now if that's your premise, what's your deduction?"

"It's not just because he isn't the type—theoretically, anyone could become a user. Gavin was on to something. He felt there was a connection between Mancini's murder and the burglary. A few hours later he calls to tell me he's had this major breakthrough—then he disappears. The next day he shows up stoned out of his mind. He may have stumbled onto something important—or was about to. I have a hunch that if he knew too much, he'd be dead. Looks more like he was getting too close and someone wanted him out of the way."

"So they discredit him by making him look like a drug user." Gram pulled her keys out of her handbag.

"Something like that."

Gram nodded. "It's plausible. In a way I wish J.B. and I weren't going back to the coast, but I do need to get home.

I have an article due for Northwest Magazine in a couple of days."

When they reached the car, Jennie remembered the interrupted conversation they'd had coming in. "You started to tell me something about Mr. Mancini earlier."

"Oh yes." Gram got into the car but didn't start it. "It's rather curious, really. Your *Mr.* Mancini is actually *Doctor* Mancini. He graduated with honors from Harvard and went on to become a chemistry professor there, then later moved to Berkeley. Seems he got a grant from a pharmaceutical company to create a new drug."

"Wow. That's impressive, but if that's the case, what was he doing at Trinity High? Why would he go from a prestigious university like Harvard to a small private school?"

"That, my dear, is precisely the question I had."

"Well, did you find out?"

"As a matter of fact, I did. It seems Dr. Mancini was asked to resign after several students reported that he had been making, selling, and using designer drugs."

# 12

Talk about bombshells. Jennie felt the impact of Gram's revelation clear down to her toes. "That sure changes things," she said above the roar of the car's engine. "Maybe Mr.—um *Doctor*—Mancini stole the supplies from the chemistry lab at Trinity and started doing the drug thing again."

"That's a possibility, but you also need to know that Dr. Mancini was never convicted. In fact, the case never went to trial."

"Why not?"

"Not enough evidence."

Jennie pondered the news. Even if Dr. Mancini had been responsible for the burglary at Trinity High, that left another big question. Who had killed him? After mulling the question over and not getting anywhere, Jennie placed it in the back of her mind with the other information she'd gleaned. She'd bring it all out and write it down, then go back over it again when she wasn't so tired. Besides, there was one more very important issue she needed to talk with Gram about.

"Gram?" Jennie began, not certain what approach to take. "I need to ask you something really important."

"Hmm—I think I know that look. Trouble at home?"

Jennie sighed. "Sort of. It's about Mom marrying Michael. I mean—I like Michael—it's just that every time I think about them getting married, I get this sick feeling in the pit of my stomach."

"Let me guess. This has something to do with your father."

"Yes. I can't stand knowing he's alive and not being able to tell Mom." Jennie glanced at her grandmother. "It isn't fair that we can't tell her. She should know before she gets married again."

"She did get a divorce."

"I know it would be legal, but that's not the problem. It just feels so wrong. Dad shouldn't be deceiving her like that. And something else—I can't help but think she might not marry Michael if she knew Dad was still alive. Maybe it's wishful thinking—but . . ."

Gram reached over and squeezed Jennie's hand. "I've given the situation a lot of thought myself. And I've talked to J.B."

"You have?"

"We both feel your father was wrong in making some of the choices he did. And to be honest, sometimes I think the government tends to be a bit more clandestine than necessary. Jason should never have put the responsibility of keeping his secret on your shoulders nor on mine. He should have found a way to tell Susan."

Even though Jennie agreed and had brought the subject up, she felt a sudden urge to defend Dad's actions. "But he was doing what he had to do to protect us. And we wouldn't have found out if I hadn't been so determined to find him. My trying to find him proved how dangerous being around him could be."

"True. I believe he did what he felt he had to do. Perhaps it's still too dangerous for him to come home, but you're absolutely right—your mother deserves to know the truth."

"So, can we tell her?"

"That's not a decision we can make on our own, and I don't think you or I should be the ones to break the news. But I have asked J.B. to talk to your father's superiors. There may be a way we can resolve the problem."

Excitement bounded through Jennie's veins as she thought of the possibilities. "Do you think I could see him again—talk to him?" *Oh, please say yes . . . please.*

"I don't know. Personally, I'd like nothing more than to see Jason come back to us—even if it is under a different persona. I do think it would be a mistake, though, for you to get your hopes up. Even if your mother is told the truth about Jason, I doubt she'd change her mind about marrying Michael. And I doubt Jason would be willing to change careers to please your mother."

"You're probably right. Mom hated his being an agent. But she's changed, Gram. She and Michael split up because he was so involved with his work. Michael is still involved, but Mom went back to him anyway." Of course, being a pastor wasn't as dangerous as being in law enforcement, but Jennie didn't want to think about that.

After a few minutes Jennie asked, "How soon will you know?"

"That's a difficult question to answer. I'll talk to J.B. again tonight."

Jennie leaned back against the seat and closed her eyes. She imagined Dad coming home and telling Mom he was still alive. Mom would be upset, of course, but she'd soon come to understand the sacrifice Dad had made. He wouldn't look like himself, either. He'd be blond, Jennie decided, with a wonderful tan from having worked in the tropics. And he'd be wearing glasses. Or maybe contacts.

Jennie thought again about Douglas. Could contacts make eyes a lighter shade of blue? Douglas had a tan. She'd look at him more closely next time she saw him. On the other hand, wouldn't he find a way to let her know if he was her father? Not necessarily.

*Don't get your hopes up, McGrady,* she reminded herself again. Not an easy task. No matter how hard she tried to block the images out, they came again and again. Dad show-ing up on the doorstep and pulling Mom into his arms. Mom telling Michael she couldn't marry him. Mom and Jennie in-troducing Nick to his real daddy. And Mom and Dad, not Mom and Michael, walking down the aisle. Jennie wondered if a person could annul a divorce the same way they annulled a marriage. That would be easier—but not as romantic.

Though she'd tried to stay awake, Jennie drifted off, com-ing to when Gram pulled into Aunt Kate's driveway and cut the engine. "We're back, dear."

Opening the car door, Jennie unfolded herself from the less than spacious front seat and stretched, rubbing the kink out of her neck at the same time.

"Are you coming in?" Gram came around the car and joined her in the driveway.

"I guess." She glanced around. The only cars parked in the driveway besides her own were Gram's T-Bird and the Calhouns' Taurus. "Looks like Mom and Nick have gone home. Wonder how Lisa's evening with Rafael went."

"I don't think you'll have to wait long to find out. From the way Lisa is grinning, I'd say the evening was a complete success."

Lisa ran down the stairs toward them. "It's about time you got here. We were getting worried. Actually, I was hoping you'd be back before Rafael had to leave. He is so wonder-ful—even our moms thought so. I can't wait for you to meet him, Gram."

Lisa spent the next five minutes filling them in on the de-tails. How Rafael didn't speak very good English and that's why he hadn't called her sooner. How he planned to become a U.S. citizen, liked the same things Lisa did, had a married sister still living in Mexico, and about a hundred or so other vital statistics.

"Hi, you two." Aunt Kate rescued them from Lisa's litany. "You're just in time for some tea. I put the kettle on just before I tucked the boys in."

"Nick's staying over?" Jennie followed her aunt and grandmother into the kitchen.

"Sure is. You're welcome to as well, Jennie. Just call your mom and let her know either way."

"I'll stay." Being with Mom and not telling her about Dad had been growing harder by the day. Now, after talking with Gram, keeping the secret would be even more difficult. Jennie picked up the phone and punched in her home phone number. It rang twice before the answering machine came on. She waited for the beep, then said, "Hi, Mom, it's me. Just wanted to tell you I'm staying over at Lisa's. I'll talk to you tomorrow."

"I take it she wasn't home," Gram said when Jennie hung up.

"Nope." Jennie glanced at her watch. "When did she leave here?"

"Shortly after you and Gram did. But don't worry. She said she was meeting someone."

"Michael?" Jennie dropped into the chair between Lisa and Gram and rested her elbows on the table.

Kate shrugged. "Probably."

"Maybe I'd better go home—make sure she's okay."

Kate came up from behind and hugged her. "You worry too much. Your mother is just fine. She was being a bit secretive—I have a hunch she and Michael wanted to spend some romantic time alone."

*Thanks, I really wanted to hear that.* Jennie's stomach was starting to hurt again. The tea helped, as did listening to Kate talk about her latest decorating job. Unfortunately the talk turned to Gavin, and Jennie felt herself getting edgy again as she and Gram brought Lisa and Kate up to date. Tomorrow she'd go back to the hospital and talk to Gavin again. Hopefully he'd have some answers.

# 13

The following morning after breakfast, Jennie packed up her little brother and Bernie and headed home. When she pulled into the empty driveway she felt a moment's panic. That subsided when Mom opened the door. Mom had parked the Oldsmobile in the garage.

Nick paused to get kissed and hugged, then broke away. "Come on, Bernie—let's find you some food."

"Clean out his dishes first," Mom yelled after him.

After a quick hug, Jennie followed her mother inside and asked how her evening with Michael had gone.

"Michael?" Mom looked confused. "Where did you get the idea I was with Michael?"

"Kate said you were meeting someone—I mean—who else would you meet?"

"Any number of people, actually." She closed the door and headed for the kitchen.

"So who was it?"

"I'd rather not talk about that just now. I'm in the middle of a project." She headed for the office. "Shouldn't take me too long—another hour."

"Mom," Jennie whined. "I hate it when you do that. Tell me. Did you find another boyfriend or something?"

"Don't take that tone with me, young lady. You're in enough trouble already."

"I'm sorry. I didn't mean to be snotty, I'm just curious."

She hauled in a deep what-am-I-going-to-do-with-you sigh. "Yes, and that curiosity is precisely what Lieutenant Rastovski and I were talking about last evening."

"You were out with Rastovski? Mom, how could you? Michael is—"

"Michael is my fiancé. And no, I'm not dating the lieutenant—nor do I intend to. We do, however, have a mutual interest in you."

Jennie plunked herself down on the chair Mom kept in her office for clients. "You were right, I don't want to know."

"He called me yesterday and asked if we could meet to discuss you—or rather your interference in the Mancini case."

Jennie winced. "I was only trying to help. He thought Mancini committed suicide—"

"And you decided to straighten him out."

"He was wrong—" Anger seeped in to replace her confusion. "Rastovski had no business talking to you about me."

"I beg your pardon." Mom's cheeks were nearly as red as her hair. "The last time I looked, you were still underage. That makes me responsible for you. And as a responsible parent I intend to keep you out of trouble."

Jennie folded her arms and clamped her jaws together. It was going to be a long day.

"Jennie, despite what you often read in mysteries or have seen on *Murder, She Wrote*," Mom went on, "police officers are not bungling idiots who'll do anything to keep from solving murder cases."

"I know that, but—"

"You also committed a crime," Mom interrupted.

"Yeah, well, so did Michael. For your information, we saved Gavin's life."

"Lieutenant Rastovski is thinking seriously about arresting both of you for obstruction of justice. He's hoping maybe that will cure you of this crazy idea you have about being a detective."

"Fine, let them arrest me. I'll call Uncle Jeff." Jeff White Cloud was Mom's brother-in-law and a lawyer.

Mom raised her hands in mock surrender, tossed Jennie a why-me look, then scooped up a folder. "You're grounded. For the next week, or until the police solve this case, you are not leaving this house."

"That's not fair! I haven't done anything wrong. Just because Rastovski says so—this was his idea, wasn't it? He wants me out of the way so he talked you into grounding me!"

"It was a mutual decision. And it isn't because he wants you out of the way. We're afraid you'll end up hurt. However, if you'd rather, I suppose I could call him and tell him you'd rather spend the time in jail."

Jennie jumped out of the chair and stalked out.

"And don't bother calling Gram. It won't do any good."

"I'll be in my room." Jennie stomped up the stairs into her room, slammed the door shut, and threw herself on the bed. After beating the bejeebers out of her pillow, she got up and paced.

A few minutes later she yanked open her desk drawer. "Oh no." Jennie watched as paper clips, pens, papers, and staples rolled and skidded over every inch of the floor. She covered her eyes and clenched her teeth. *Chill out, McGrady*, she told herself. *Take a deep breath and count to ten.* Jennie fell back onto her bed and closed her eyes. In between numbers, she had a few words with God.

*One* "I think you should know, I am not happy about this. But then I guess you can see that, can't you?"

*Two* "Why are you letting them get away with this? I mean, it's not like I've done anything all that bad. What was I supposed to do, let them kill Gavin?"

*Three* "Are you trying to tell me something here? Gram

says I should find good in everything. That isn't easy."

*Four* "I can't just forget about Mancini's murder—or Gavin."

*Five* "I suppose I could use the time by myself to make a chart. And I do have the telephone. I can make some phone calls."

Jennie skipped the remaining five numbers and hurriedly picked the stuff up from the floor and put it away. After a much-needed shower and a change of clothes, she picked up a blue spiral notebook and pen, climbed into the window seat, and began jotting down notes to herself. She began with a journal entry in which she wrote every detail she could remember, from her first contact with Mancini to the present.

Then, turning a fresh piece of paper sideways, she started her chart, making five columns, and labeling them Suspect, Motive, Means, Opportunity, and Clues. To the far left she wrote *1) Alexis Mancini.* Under Motive—*money and freedom,* but as she remembered what Lisa had said about Brian Stone, Alex's boyfriend, she added *revenge.* Jennie left the Opportunity column blank. She'd have to find out later whether or not Alex had an alibi. Under Clues, Jennie listed the trip to Europe and how Alex seemed almost glad that her stepfather was dead.

She listed Mrs. Mancini next and placed a star beside the name. Jennie wanted to have a nice little chat with her too. Under Clues she wrote: *Dr. Mancini's wife—planned his funeral and a trip to Europe on the same day.*

Brian Stone came next, then Curtis Bolton. She still hadn't had a chance to talk to Curtis or Brian either, but Jennie hoped to remedy that soon. Maybe she'd call them.

After thumbing through the phone directory, Jennie dialed Brian Stone's number. His mother answered. No, Brian wasn't there, but he'd be home after six. "Can I take a message?"

"This is Jennie McGrady—could you have him call me? My number is—"

"What's this in regard to?" Mrs. Stone's voice turned razor sharp.

"Um—" What could she say? She didn't want to lie. On the other hand, she couldn't tell her what she really wanted.

"Never mind. I think I know what you're up to. You want to ask him about Mr. Mancini's death. For your information, Jennie McGrady, Brian had nothing to do with it. He was working that day. It's bad enough that the police have been hammering away at him, but to have his schoolmates—wait a minute. Did the police put you up to this?"

"No, I—I was at the school when Michael found the body. I heard about Brian's trouble with Dr. Mancini and—"

"That information was strictly confidential." Her voice went up another octave and Jennie flinched. "My son is not a murderer. Like I told the police, the incident is in the past. Brian will be going to another school next year where they have a more flexible teaching staff."

After mumbling an apology for bothering her, Jennie hung up and scribbled out Brian's name on her suspect list. "This is stupid." Jennie tossed the notebook to the floor and let the pen drop beside it. "You don't know what you're doing, McGrady. For all you know, the murderer could be some drug pusher who didn't like the deal Mancini was cutting him." If the accusations against Dr. Mancini were true, that certainly was a possibility.

From what Rocky had told her about the manufacturing of illegal drugs, the idea made a lot of sense. Which, of course, meant the suspect list would be endless. So why was she even bothering?

Jennie's gaze drifted outside and down the quiet street they lived on. A patrol car came to a stop at the end of the street, then turned onto Magnolia. She wondered if it might be Rocky. The car pulled up to the curb in front of Jennie's house. Officer Phelps got out. A few seconds later, another car came up behind her. An officer Jennie didn't recognize joined Phelps on the street then started walking up the driveway.

Normally, Jennie wasn't afraid of the police. Yet at the moment, her stomach churned, then tied itself into one huge knot. Maybe it was what Rastovski had said about arresting her. No, he was just trying to scare her. Wasn't he?

When she heard the doorbell ring, Jennie took a deep breath and let it out slowly. *For Pete's sake, McGrady, relax. They probably just want to ask some more questions.*

"Jennie," Mom called. "There's someone here to see you."

"Coming." Jennie descended the stairs, trying to act as nonchalant about the officers' visit as possible.

"Hi." Jennie gripped the railing, willing herself to stay calm.

They waited until she reached the main floor before speaking. "Sorry to bother you, Mrs. McGrady," Officer Phelps said. "This is Officer Kelly." Phelps glanced at Mom, then back to Jennie. "But we got a tip that your daughter has been dealing drugs."

"What? You're kidding, right?" Jennie's knees threatened to buckle.

"I'm afraid not," Officer Kelly said. "Would you mind if we looked around?"

"Yes, as a matter of fact I do." Mom gripped the door.

"It's okay, Mom. I don't have anything to hide."

"In that case, you won't mind if we take a look at your car." Phelps spoke this time.

Jennie felt like a mouse being stalked by two hungry cats as she retrieved her keys from the hook in the kitchen and led the officers out to the Mustang. She unlocked the car door and stepped back while Kelly methodically searched the car.

"I don't understand this." Jennie brushed damp bangs

from her forehead. "Why would anyone—"

"Looks like we hit pay dirt." Kelly emerged from the backseat holding up a quart-sized plastic bag.

Jennie gasped and shook her head. "I—I didn't."

Phelps reached behind her and pulled out a pair of handcuffs. In the next second, Phelps spun Jennie around and pressed her against the trunk of the Mustang. She slapped the cuffs on her wrists. "You are under arrest for possession of narcotics—"

# 14

"—whatever you say can and will be held against you in a court of law."

"Wait a minute." Mom tried to grab the arresting officer's arm. Kelly held her back. "You can't just come into our home and—"

"Mrs. McGrady," Phelps said. "I know this must come as a shock to you, but it happens all the time."

"This is insane. Jennie would never—"

Officer Phelps leveled a steady gaze on Mom. "We just found a stash of methamphetamine in your daughter's car. Right where the Winslow boy said it would be."

"Gavin?" Jennie looked from one officer to the other. "That's impossible."

"Let's go. You'll have a chance to tell your story later." Phelps grasped Jennie's arm.

"No." Jennie jerked away. "You can't arrest me. Mom—" She looked back as the officers led her down the driveway. "Don't let them do this. You know I don't do drugs. Tell them."

"It's all right, Jennie." Mom seemed to have regained control while Jennie was quickly losing hers. "I'll get someone to watch Nick and be right down. Don't say anything until we get a lawyer."

"Does Rocky know about this?" Jennie asked as she let

Phelps guide her to the squad car.

"If you mean Officer Rockwell, I doubt it. He's working swing today."

"Well, call him. Tell him what's going on. He knows I wouldn't—"

"Get into the car." Officer Phelps opened the back door.

Ducking her head, Jennie folded herself inside and cringed when the door shut. Her breath came in short gasps that turned to sobs.

*Don't you dare cry, McGrady.* Jennie fought to keep her tears at bay. *You are not going to fall apart. You're not!*

On the way to the station, Phelps glanced frequently into the rearview mirror but didn't speak. For some reason Phelps didn't like her, and Jennie couldn't imagine why. She wondered briefly if the officer had planted the evidence but quickly shrugged off the notion—what possible reason could she have?

Jennie hauled in a shuddering sigh, then forced herself to take deep breaths. *Calm down, McGrady. You'll get through this. You've been in worse scrapes.* Still, she offered up a silent prayer, wishing there was something she could say or do to turn things around. But what could she say? She was being set up. If the police really had found drugs in her car, someone had planted them. But Gavin? Was that what he'd been doing in her car when she found him? Why? The questions haunted her all the way downtown.

Rocky was at the station when Phelps brought her in. His eyes narrowed when he saw her. "Devon, what's going on?" His gaze shifted from Jennie to Phelps.

"What are you doing here? Thought you said you were off today." Officer Phelps deposited Jennie in a chair.

"I am. Her mother called me."

Phelps harrumphed. "And you hot-foot it down here to be with her in her hour of need. How touching." In the look that passed between Rocky and Phelps, Jennie finally figured out what was going on. Devon Phelps was jealous. Somehow she'd gotten the idea that Jennie and Rocky were an item. How funny. Not that Jennie hadn't had her moments. Sometimes she still wished Rocky were younger—or that she was a little older—but mostly, she was just glad to have him as a friend.

"It isn't what you think—" Rocky ran a hand through his sandy hair. "Look, we'll talk about that later. In the meantime, I suggest you lighten up." He nodded toward Jennie. "What have you got on her?"

"Your little would-be cop seems to think she's above the law. Found a bag of ice stashed under the seat of her car."

"Tell her I'm innocent, Rocky." Jennie's pleading dark eyes searched for some kind of empathy from him. "You know I wouldn't do anything like that. Besides, I'm not stupid. Do you really think that if I were into drugs I'd leave the stuff in my car?"

"What tipped you off?" Rocky ignored Jennie's pleas.

"The Winslow kid confessed this morning. Told us she might have been the one who drugged him. Says someone knocked him out. Doesn't remember much after that."

"He's lying. I'd never do anything like that. Rocky, tell her." She may as well have been invisible for all the attention Rocky and Devon Phelps were paying to her. They moved a few feet away from her and lowered their voices so she couldn't hear.

Jennie tipped her head back in exasperation and whacked the wall. "Ouch." Great, now she had a headache to go along with everything else. How could Gavin have implicated her like that? Why would he lie?

"Fine," Phelps said in a voice loud enough for Jennie to hear. "You can talk to her while I'm doing my report. Rastovski and Douglas want to question her too, so you can call them in when you're finished."

"You heading back out?" Rocky asked.

"Yeah—we got a shooting down on the waterfront. It's a mess down there." Officer Phelps paused beside Jennie long enough to remove the handcuffs, then left.

"Let's go someplace where we can talk." Rocky grabbed her by the elbow and pulled her up.

Jennie dutifully followed Rocky down a long hall and into a small room that was sparsely furnished with a scarred wooden library table and four mismatched chairs. An interrogation room, Jennie decided. "Is someone watching from the other room?"

Rocky glanced up at the mirror and shrugged. "I doubt it. I'm not acting in an official capacity at the moment. What you say to me you say as a friend." He pulled out a chair away from a long rectangular table. "Have a seat. Want something to drink? Water, Coke?"

Jennie shook her head. "Maybe later. Um—am I supposed to be fingerprinted or something?"

"Yeah—but I'd like to hear what happened first."

Some of the knots in Jennie's stomach had come undone, and she was beginning to relax. Mom would be there soon with a lawyer and she'd be released. And when she was, she planned to have a long talk with Gavin Winslow.

Rocky sat on the edge of the table.

"You believe me, don't you? I've never used drugs. And I never would."

"There's a lot of money in the drug business. Not all dealers are users."

Jennie's jaw dropped. "You can't be serious. I'm on your side, remember?"

His blue gaze caught hers. "I know, Jennie. You got any ideas on how and when the meth got in your car?"

Jennie rubbed her forehead trying to remember. "Yesterday at the school. I forgot to lock my car. Gavin crawled into the backseat." Jennie broke eye contact and stared at a jagged *A* someone had carved into the table. "Gavin must have planted the drugs there, but I can't understand why. He doesn't do drugs either. At least I don't think so."

"Look, Jennie, I don't know if you realize it, but you're in a lot of trouble here."

"I didn't *do* anything. Why can't you believe me?"

"What I believe doesn't matter. What counts here is the evidence. Unfortunately, this drug thing is only the tip of the iceberg. You're also a suspect in Mancini's murder."

"B-but that's crazy!" Jennie sputtered. "I'm the one who convinced Rastovski the case wasn't a suicide."

Rocky's blue gaze settled on her again. "I told you all your snooping around would get you into trouble one of these days. Rastovski thinks you know too much to be an innocent bystander. And now, with the Winslow kid fingering you as one of his assailants . . ."

"Couldn't you talk to him?"

"I have. Rastovski is fairly new to the department. He's a good cop—at least that's what we've been told. The guy's got a reputation for being a bulldog. Right now he's sniffing around, looking for suspects, possible connections. He'll circle around until he's sure he's got a case before he makes an arrest."

Jennie leaned her elbows on the table and buried her face in her hands. "What am I going to do? How can I convince him I'm innocent?"

"Tell him everything you know. If it makes you feel any better, I think he's leaning more toward Michael than you. Did you know your future stepfather and Mancini almost came to blows—about an hour before the shooting? Any idea what they might have been arguing about?"

Jennie straightened. Though she suspected Michael had been protecting Brian Stone, she didn't know for certain. "I—I can't imagine Michael fighting with anyone. Why are you asking me—I mean, why not just ask Michael?"

Rocky sighed. "He's not talking. Says the object of his

discussion with Mancini has nothing to do with the case and he won't break a confidence."

"Maybe I could talk to him."

Jennie never did hear Rocky's reply. The door opened and Rastovski and Douglas walked in, followed by Mom and a guy Jennie recognized as one of Trinity's board members.

Mom leaned over to hug Jennie. "I got here as quickly as I could, sweetheart." Her glance darted from her daughter to the man who now had his briefcase open on the table. "You remember Mr. Collins? He's an attorney."

"Hi, Jennie." He smiled and stretched a hand toward Jennie. After a quick handshake, he dropped his gaze to the briefcase, pulled out a yellow legal pad and pen, and sat down.

For the next few minutes, Jennie felt like she may as well have been on another planet. They spoke in a jargon she barely understood and acted as though she didn't exist. Which was okay with her as long as the charges were dropped and she could leave.

Unfortunately, that didn't happen. Rastovski turned away from the lawyer, slammed a fist on the table, and walked out. "Book her."

Jennie nearly bit through her lower lip. This couldn't be happening. She took a deep breath and turned to the lawyer.

"Why are they booking me? What did you say to him to make him mad?"

Mr. Collins glanced up from his note taking and met her tearful gaze head on. "I just told him that questioning you would be pointless."

"But won't that make me look guilty? Call him back. I'll tell him everything I know." Jennie stood and aimed for the door. "I don't want to go to jail."

"You won't. Since this is your first offense, they'll process you and with any luck we'll have you back home by dinner."

"My first offense? What do you mean? You don't think I'm guilty, do you?"

"They do have some compelling evidence, Jennie. But, like I said, in all probability you won't even have to stand trial. I think we can plea bargain and get you off with community service."

"Community—wait a minute. Why would I have to do anything? I'm innocent."

He sighed. "That may be. It's a rather complicated situation, but our chances are much better if the case doesn't go to trial."

"Honey, please." Mom grasped Jennie's shoulder. "For once, just do as you're told. Mr. Collins knows what he's doing."

Jennie glanced at Rocky, who was still leaning against the wall next to Douglas. His eyes were narrow slits devoid of compassion. Another officer stepped into the room and escorted Jennie away.

Feeling about as helpless as a piece of toilet paper, Jennie finally gave up and let the authorities flush her through their bureaucratic system.

Hours later, Jennie walked out of the station and ducked into her mom's Oldsmobile. They didn't speak for the first few minutes. Jennie stole several quick glances to determine Mom's mood. She wasn't mad, Jennie decided, but she wasn't too happy either.

"Well," Jennie said after another few minutes of silence, "aren't you going to lecture me?"

Mom frowned, taking her eyes off the road for a moment. "What for? You said you didn't do it, and I believe you."

"Oh." Jennie sank back against the seat. She supposed she should have said thanks, or some such thing. But at the moment Jennie didn't trust herself to say anything for fear the lump in her throat would dislodge and reduce her to tears.

"What we're going to have to find out," Mom continued, "is why Gavin Winslow would lie about your involvement. I've talked to Maddie and she's very upset."

Jennie leaned forward wondering if she'd heard right. "With me or Gavin?"

"Gavin, of course. She believes you too."

"So are we going to the hospital?"

"Yes. Maddie's meeting us there."

———

"Susan, Jennie . . ." Maddie hugged each of them when they stepped off the elevator. "Thanks so much for coming."

Maddie led them to a small waiting room. Jennie paused at the door and looked down the empty hallway. Gavin's room was several doors down. She wanted nothing more than to march into Gavin's room and confront him. The only thing that stopped her was a slight pressure against her arm where Maddie had placed her hand.

"You can go in to see him in a few minutes," she whispered, "but I need to talk to you first."

After pouring herself and Mom coffee from a large pot on the counter at the far end of the room, Maddie sat on the edge of a maroon chair. She took a sip and grimaced. "It's hard to know where to begin. I suppose I should start with an apology. Jennie, I'm so sorry Gavin involved you in all of this."

"Me too." Jennie stared at a wrinkle on her white cotton shorts. "Any idea why he did?"

Maddie shook her head. "He's terribly confused."

"That's for sure. It's almost like he's been programmed or something."

Maddie's head snapped up. "Programmed. Jennie, you may be right. I wrote a book a couple of years ago based on a true story about a sixteen-year-old girl who left home and joined this bizarre religious sect. A private detective agency finally found her, but all they could do was let the parents know she was safe. Her twin, who is a lot like you, Jennie, went undercover and joined the group to get her sister out. The thing is, this girl had been programmed to believe in all kinds of terrible things. They called themselves The True Believers and claimed to be Christians, but nearly everything they did opposed the Christian faith. They executed hate crimes against people of other races. They all shaved their heads and acted much like some of the extreme groups we see today—only they were into sacrifices—let's just say they didn't always stop with animals."

Mom shook her head. "I get so tired of that sort of thing. These extremists get all the press and give anyone who believes in God a bad rap."

"Tell me about it." Maddie took another sip of coffee. "It's almost embarrassing to call myself a Christian anymore. There are so many radicals out there doing horrible things in God's name."

"Well, there really isn't much we can do about it except show people that Christ's message is love, not hate."

Uh-oh. The two things you never wanted to get Mom discussing were politics and religion. She could go on for hours debating issues. Jennie had a hunch if she didn't stop them, they'd be there all day. "Um, Maddie," Jennie interrupted, trying to get the conversation back on track. "Is there any way to tell if Gavin was programmed?"

"What—oh, I don't know. I'll talk to a psychologist friend of mine and find out."

Mom looked at the dark liquid in her cup, then at Jennie. "I think it's obvious that Gavin was either programmed or coerced into naming Jennie as a drug dealer. The question I have is why."

"I've been asking myself the same thing." Maddie set her half-empty cup on a coffee table. "The only possible answer is that someone wants both Jennie and Gavin out of the way."

"And if that's the case, we need to ask ourselves who."

Jennie shuddered. Even though she'd been asking the same questions herself, it seemed more frightening to hear it out loud. *I think the who is obvious.* Jennie thought the response but didn't say it. *The only person Gavin and I are a threat to is the person who tried to make Mancini's murder look like a suicide.*

Jennie's gaze drifted from her mother to Maddie. The two were now talking in hushed voices and acting as if Jennie had faded into the woodwork. She thought about reminding them she was still there but didn't. It seemed strange to see them—especially Mom—talking about the case as if they planned to get involved.

Not so unusual, maybe. Mom could be pretty intense at times—especially when her children were in jeopardy. On occasion the mild-mannered bookkeeper would shed her cautious and inhibited lifestyle and slip into what Jennie called her "wonder woman" role. A smile tugged at the corner of Jennie's mouth. In some ways Mom and Dad had more in common than Mom cared to admit.

Jennie cleared her throat and stood up. "I'm going to see Gavin now."

Maddie and Mom looked up at her then at each other. "Oh, I'm sorry, Jennie," Maddie said. "We didn't mean to exclude you. By all means, go see Gavin. He had a couple of friends with him. Ray left about fifteen minutes ago—Curtis may be gone as well."

"Ray—Curtis?" The names went through her like an electric impulse, jerking the hairs on the back of her neck to attention.

"Yes." Maddie smiled. "Curtis Bolton and his brother Ray."

Jennie's feet seemed to have glued themselves to the floor. "I didn't know they were friends."

"Oh my, yes. Curtis and Gavin have been close friends

since kindergarten. The Boltons live about half a mile from us. The poor boy is devastated about what's happened. He was Mr. Mancini's lab assistant, you know. And then to have his best friend shot." Maddie paused for a moment. "Actually, Jennie, I just had a thought. You might want to talk to Curtis. Maybe you can cheer him up."

"I'll—um—I'll see what I can do." Jennie managed to get her feet moving again and practically ran out the door. She couldn't believe it. Why hadn't Gavin mentioned that Curtis was his friend? She wanted to talk to him all right, but cheering him up wasn't on her agenda.

# 15

Curtis was just coming out of Gavin's room when Jennie started down the hall. He smiled when he saw her. He'd grown since she'd last seen him. Last year they were the same height—now she had to look up to meet his gaze. He'd filled out some—lost that awkward, gangly adolescent look. In fact, with his long blond hair and baby blues, he looked like a model for those steamy novels Mom wouldn't let her read. Not that she wanted to. Lisa had sneaked one once and assured Jennie it hadn't been worth the bother. One thing for sure, Curtis Bolton had turned into a total babe. Especially when he smiled. No wonder Lisa had remembered him so easily.

"Hi, Jennie." He stopped in front of her. "I was hoping I'd run in to you. In fact, I planned to call you tonight." Curtis stuffed his hands in the pockets of his cutoffs. "I—um—heard about what happened—to you, I mean—getting arrested and all."

"How'd you hear about it so quickly? I was just released about an hour ago and I know it didn't make the news."

"Maddie told me. Funny, I never figured you or Gavin for getting involved in drugs."

"I am not involved in anything." Jennie had so much to talk to Curtis about, she didn't know where to begin. She glanced toward Gavin's room. "How is he?"

126

"Sleeping right now. Poor guy's really been through it."

"Haven't we all? Did he tell you anything?"

Curtis shook his head. "Nothing coherent."

"Actually, I've been wanting to talk to you too. Maybe you could come by the house later—after dinner."

"Tonight?" Curtis's gaze darted to the floor and back up to her face. From his surprised expression you'd have thought she'd suggested meeting him on the moon.

"It doesn't have to be tonight—if you're busy—"

"Um—no. I was going to do something with my brother, but—" His grin slipped back into place. "Tonight's fine."

"Are you sure?"

He nodded and took a step back. "Seven okay?"

"Fine." Jennie watched as he turned around and headed back in the same direction he'd come. A second or two later, he stopped and headed back toward her. "Wrong way." He laughed at his mistake and hurried past, then ducked into the waiting room, probably to say goodbye to Maddie. *Curious*, Jennie mused. *Wonder what he was so flustered about?*

Jennie slipped into Gavin's room and sat in a chair that had been pulled over to the bed. She'd been furious with him all day, but now, watching him sleep, she felt sorry for him. His forehead wrinkled and he arched his back as if he were in pain or having a bad dream.

His eyes flew open and collided with hers.

Jennie grasped the bed rail and pulled herself up. "I'm sorry I frightened you. I—"

"No," he gasped. "Stay away from me. They'll kill you."

"What?" She backed off a bit and lifted her hands to show him they were empty. "You're not making any sense. Just settle down. I'm not going to hurt you."

Gavin grabbed the trapeze above his head, his face contorted with pain. "Just go away. Please. I can't talk to you."

"Gavin, it's okay. I'm here." Maddie stepped in front of

Jennie. "Shh. It's all right, sweetheart. Jennie just came by to say hi. She's your friend."

"No," he whimpered like a small child. "Keep her away from me."

"Okay—just settle down. She's leaving now." Maddie glanced apologetically at Jennie.

"I-I'm sorry," Jennie stammered as she backed out of the room.

"Oh, man, it hurts so bad."

"I'll have the nurse bring you something for pain." Maddie pressed the button on the call light.

Outside the room, Jennie leaned against the wall and closed her eyes. Her heart hammered against her chest. Tears gathered behind her eyelids.

"Honey—" Mom's arms went around Jennie in an attempt to comfort her.

"Don't." Jennie pulled away and headed down the hall. "Let's just go home, okay?"

"Do you want to talk about it?" Mom joined Jennie in the car ten minutes later.

"No." Jennie folded her arms across her chest.

"Maddie told me what he said to you. You have to understand, Jennie, Gavin doesn't know what he's doing." She started the car and put it in reverse.

"Doesn't he?" Jennie glanced at Mom, then turned to look out the side window. "What if he does? What if he's in on it and is just trying to throw the police off the track by blaming me and acting crazy?"

"Jennie . . ."

"Well, it's possible."

"Maddie and I believe both you and Gavin are innocent of any wrongdoing—except maybe being a little too nosy for your own good."

"How can you know for sure? A lot of parents say they

can't believe their kids could do drugs. Lots of times they're wrong."

"Ever hear of intuition?"

"Of course."

"Well, my intuition is usually right on where you're concerned. Unfortunately, I don't always pay close enough attention. When you're in trouble, I can feel it. I know when you are being honest with me and when you're not. And Jennie, trust me on this. If you were to ever experiment with drugs, which I doubt you would, I'd know. Deep inside, I'd know."

*Do you know about Dad too?* Jennie wanted to ask. *Do you know I'm keeping a secret from you?* "So, it's like you can read my mind?"

"Not exactly. I just know when something is bothering you. Like with your father."

Jennie snapped to attention.

"What about him?"

Mom shook her head. "I'm not sure. I keep hoping someday you'll talk about it and let me know how you really feel. You're putting up a good front. I can tell you're hesitant about my marrying Michael. There's just an unsettled feeling about it. I can sense it in you—and in myself for that matter."

"Does that mean you're having second thoughts?" *Oh, Mom, say yes—please say yes.*

"Sometimes I hear this voice in my head saying not to marry him—other times I feel like it's the right thing to do." Her shoulders rose and fell. She glanced at Jennie for a second, setting her shimmering red hair in motion. Her somber expression gave way to a smile. "I wonder if one can ever feel sure about decisions like this."

"Maybe you should wait awhile, then."

"Hmm. Michael and I talked this afternoon. I'd called to tell him what happened. He thinks we should postpone the wedding at least until this business with the murder is over.

I guess maybe that's why I'm having second thoughts again. He's been impossible lately."

"Like how?"

"Jumpy, irritable. He's protecting someone, and that concerns me."

"Rocky said something about that. Did you know Michael is a suspect?"

Mom nodded. "Lieutenant Rastovski told me. He and that DEA agent questioned me for about an hour this afternoon while you were being processed."

"Did they tell you I was a suspect in the murder case too?"

"Yes, but I think I convinced them you had nothing to do with the murder."

"And the drugs?"

Mom bit her lip. "I'm not sure about that."

Jennie forced her thoughts back to Gavin. "It was really weird, Mom—what Gavin said, I mean."

"I should say so. Whatever happened to him must have been terrifying to have him react to you the way he did."

"What he said didn't make sense. At first I thought maybe he was afraid of me. While I was waiting for you in the car, I wrote down what he said—word for word. Listen to this." Jennie reached into the backseat for the pad and read, "First he looks at me like he is seeing a ghost, then he says, *No— Stay away from me. They'll kill you.* I tried to calm him down, but he wouldn't listen. Then he says, *Just go away. Please. I can't talk to you.* Doesn't that sound strange to you? Like, if he was really scared of me, why wouldn't he say something like, 'Don't kill me'? And it seems like he would have said 'I don't *want* to talk to you,' instead of *'I can't.'* "

"I admit it does seem a bit odd, but Maddie did say he was confused. He's still on pain medication."

"I know, but I got this feeling." Jennie tossed her mother a grin. "Intuition. Anyway, I got to wondering if maybe

Gavin isn't as confused as everybody thinks. Maybe he wasn't scared *of* me, but *for* me."

"I don't follow."

"Okay." Jennie twisted sideways and loosened the seat belt. "Gavin disappears. The next day he shows up stoned out of his mind. Let's say our intuition is right and he doesn't do drugs. That means someone abducted him and drugged him. Why would they do that? Because he knows too much? Because he's a threat?"

"Why didn't they just kill him?" Mom frowned. "Did you hear what I just said? I can't believe I would have such a cold-blooded thought."

"That, my dear mother, is an excellent point. Maybe the murderer isn't a cold-blooded killer. Maybe he—or she—didn't mean to kill Dr. Mancini. Mancini may have interrupted a second burglary and the thief got scared. Thing is, this person might not want to kill again but has to do something to keep from being caught."

"All right, go on."

Jennie hesitated. It seemed strange to be having this kind of discussion with Mom. "I will, but first I gotta ask you a question."

"Sure."

"Why are you letting me talk about this? You grounded me this morning for getting involved."

Mom pulled into their driveway and turned off the car. Silence stretched between them. Mom finally broke it. "That's a difficult question. Let's talk about it over an iced tea."

A few minutes later, Jennie tapped her foot against the floor, sending the front porch swing into motion.

Mom pressed the frosty glass to her flushed cheeks. "Bet we'll have a thunderstorm tonight. Hot and muggy afternoons like this usually bring them on."

Jennie peered at the hazy blue sky and pushed her damp

bangs off her forehead. "Am I still grounded?"

"No." Mom stared at the amber liquid in her glass. "I overreacted, Jennie, and I apologize. Lieutenant Rastovski frightened me. Keeping you locked up isn't going to solve anything. While I was waiting for you at the police station this afternoon, I got to thinking back to a conversation I had with Joseph White Cloud."

Joseph was Uncle Jeff's father—a Nez Perce Indian and just about the wisest man Jennie had ever met. There'd been a murder at the dude ranch the White Clouds owned—and a major land dispute. Joseph had actually supported her efforts to solve the crime.

"Joseph reminded me that it was in your nature to solve puzzles," Mom went on. "He said you had a wonderful mind and that I should cherish your gifts rather than keep you from using them. He said I should trust you more and be thankful that strong will of yours seeks to do good and not evil."

Jennie lifted the glass to her mouth, not trusting herself to speak. She could almost hear the old man's voice in her mother's words and see his wrinkled face as he must have looked when he'd spoken them.

"Don't get the wrong idea, though, Jennie. I'm not giving you *carte blanche*."

Jennie frowned. "What's that?"

"A blank check—in other words, you can't do anything you want to. All I'm saying is that I'll try to be more understanding and maybe work with you instead of against you."

For the next few minutes they drank their tea in the quiet of the late afternoon. With Nick and Bernie staying overnight with Kurt again, the place was almost too quiet.

"So," Mom said, setting her glass on the white wicker table, "tell me more about this theory of yours on Gavin's abduction."

"It isn't much of a theory so far, just a clue—like a piece of the puzzle. See, the way a mystery works, Mom, is you look

132

for clues, ask questions, and gather information from as many sources as possible. Pretty soon you have a lot of pieces. Some fit, others don't. You just keep working at it and hope that it will eventually come together."

"You said Gavin might have been afraid *for* you rather than *of* you. If you're right, that means whoever went after Gavin could come after you next."

"Or they may have used Gavin to get me out of the way."

"How so?"

"They have Gavin plant drugs in my car and somehow get him to name me as a drug dealer. Maybe they figure I'll be so busy getting myself out of trouble I won't have time to think about the murder. It accomplished something else too. Having the police thinking I'm involved in drugs pretty much shoots my credibility—and Gavin's too."

"Hmm. Yours maybe, but not mine or Maddie's."

"What are you saying? You can't—"

"Get involved? Honey, we already are. We have children who, for some reason, have been accused of crimes they didn't commit. The police aren't the least bit interested in clearing your names, but we are. Can't have you two applying to Harvard or Yale with a criminal record, now, can we?"

"But it's too—"

"Dangerous? I don't think so. Maddie and I will be very discreet." Mom's green eyes sparked with determination.

The telephone rang and Mom hurried to answer it. Jennie managed to get her gaping mouth closed and followed her inside. *This is all a sick joke, McGrady,* Jennie told herself. *Mom is just playing some kind of mind game. Reverse psychology. She probably just wants you to know how it feels when you pull stuff like that on her.* But what if it wasn't? What if Mom and Maddie really did plan to get involved? Mom didn't know the first thing about solving crimes, and Jennie doubted that Maddie did either. She had to find a way to stop them before they got hurt.

# 16

"Sure, I guess that would be okay. We're just having a salad and bread, but . . ." After a few seconds Mom hung up the phone and turned around and headed for the refrigerator. A frown creased her forehead.

"Who was that?"

"Lieutenant Rastovski. He just invited himself to dinner."

Jennie grimaced. "He wants to question me, I'll bet. Without the lawyer."

"I don't think so." Mom opened the refrigerator door and closed it again.

"You don't think he's coming to arrest me, do you?"

"No. I don't know why, but I have this awful feeling it has something to do with Michael."

A short time later, Lieutenant Rastovski, frowning and intense, sat at the dining room table shoveling Mom's Chinese chicken salad into his mouth like he hadn't eaten in a week.

"I—ah—I'm sorry I don't have anything more substantial to offer you," Mom said. "I had planned on having trout, but—"

"This is fine, thanks. I appreciate getting a chance to eat. All I've had today is coffee. Not good, Mrs. McGrady. This case has been driving me crazy."

"Oh?" Mom speared a piece of lettuce and lifted it to her mouth.

"I keep goin' around in circles. Got too many suspects and not enough solid evidence." He guzzled down half a glass of milk and reached for another slice of sourdough bread. "One of those suspects is your fiancé."

"Which is nonsense. I told you yesterday that Michael had nothing to do with that teacher's murder."

"We ran a background check on Rhodes—came up clean—no priors."

*"He's one of the good guys,"* Jennie remembered her father saying shortly after she'd found him. They were in a speed boat cruising back to Cozumel. *"Michael will make a good husband for your mother and a good father to you and Nick. Be nice to him, Jennie. He's one of the good guys."* She'd wanted so much to have Dad tell her he was coming home. But he couldn't give her false hope. Dad had another mission. He always had another mission.

"How long have you known him, Mrs. McGrady?"

"Um—seven, eight months now. We met at a Christmas party at church last year."

"Love at first sight?" The sharp tone in his voice brought Jennie out of her daydream.

Jennie glanced up at him and groaned inwardly. *Oh no, not another one.* Rastovski was jealous. Mom was becoming far too popular.

"No." Mom pushed a piece of chicken around on her plate. "We were attracted to each other, but—" Mom took a deep breath. "Lieutenant, is this really necessary?"

"I need to know as much as possible about Michael Rhodes, Mrs. McGrady. We have some compelling evidence connecting him to his co-worker's murder." Rastovski's expression softened. "I know this is difficult for you, but necessary."

Jennie's heart did a double flip. *Oh no.* Jennie backed out of the thought the moment it hit her. Like a dead-end street it would lead to nowhere.

"I—um—I'll take care of the dishes," Jennie stammered, eager to get away and get a grip.

Neither of them seemed to notice as she gathered the plates and headed for the kitchen. After setting the plates on the counter, Jennie stood in the kitchen for a few minutes, willing the wild fantasy of Mom and Lieutenant Rastovski getting married out of her head. Mom was in love with Michael. She shouldn't really be interested in either man—in case Dad ever came back.

"That's stupid," Jennie muttered. She felt like marching right back into the dining room and announcing to her mother that she had no business being so pretty and—Jennie shook her head. That was even dumber. *What's the matter with you, McGrady?* Maybe being arrested had damaged her brain. She sure was having trouble thinking clearly.

Jennie squared her shoulders and went back into the dining room. Mom and Lieutenant Rastovski were heading out to the porch. Jennie watched them through the bay window, hoping he'd leave. No such luck. They settled into the porch swing—both of them—together—their shoulders almost touching. Rastovski had dropped the Mrs. and was calling her Susan.

Jennie couldn't name the jumble of emotions clamoring around inside her. She had no idea what to do or say. With robotic movements, Jennie finished clearing off the table, listening to bits and pieces of Mom's and Rastovski's conversation as the sounds drifted into the open window and screen door. She washed and dried the table and replaced the tablecloth and colorful dahlia centerpiece.

Mom was talking about Dad now, and Jennie wondered how and why they'd made the transition from Michael.

"Jason was a good man," Mom said. "But I think his priorities were misplaced. I suppose I shouldn't judge him so

136

harshly, but I never could understand why he felt so strongly about staying in a field that took him away from his family so much."

Not wanting to hear any more negative garbage about Dad, Jennie wandered into the kitchen and made a pitcher of lemonade. Curtis would be there in less than half an hour. The thought did nothing to settle her churning stomach. Jennie considered him a suspect and had a hunch the police did as well.

She poured lemonade into two tall glasses, dropped in straws, and carried them out to Mom and the lieutenant. Rastovski was gone.

"When did he leave?" Jennie asked. "I didn't hear his car."

"About five minutes ago." She took the drink Jennie handed her. "Thanks. He had to respond to a call."

"He likes you."

"I know." Mom ducked her head. A fat tear dripped down and landed on Mom's hand.

"What's wrong?"

"I wish I knew. Jennie, I feel so foolish and confused."

Jennie eased onto the empty spot on the swing, wishing she could think of something appropriate to say.

"I like him too. It's the strangest thing." Mom ran a hand through her thick mop of natural curls, made even more curly by the humidity. "This can't be happening," she groaned. "I'm an engaged woman. I'm not supposed to be attracted to other men. What am I going to tell Michael?"

"M-maybe you shouldn't tell him anything. At least not yet. Remember how you thought you liked Mr. Evans and you and Michael broke up? After a while, you realized you didn't love Frank. Maybe it'll be the same with Lieutenant Rastovski."

"You make me sound like—never mind. I was going to say adolescent, but you're an adolescent and at the moment you seem to be much more rational than I am. Maybe I'm going through a midlife crisis."

*You sure are going through something.* "Mom?"

"What?"

"I forgot to tell you earlier, but there's a guy from school coming over in a few minutes. A friend of Gavin's."

"The one that was visiting Gavin while we were at the hospital?"

"Yeah. Curtis Bolton."

"And you'd like me to get lost, right?"

"Well, I do want to ask him some questions, and he's more likely to talk to me if my mother isn't hanging around."

"He seemed like a very nice young man—and very handsome. Maddie and I were both wishing we were a few years younger."

"Mo-ther!"

"I'm just kidding, sweetheart." Mom stood up just as a guy on a motorcycle cornered Elm and Magnolia, going at least ten miles over the posted twenty-five miles per hour. His tires screeched as he turned into the driveway. "Oh, dear," Mom muttered under her breath. "Tell me that isn't him."

"Sorry, Mom."

Curtis pulled off his helmet, shaking loose a mass of gold curls. Settling the helmet on his Harley, he waved at Jennie and started toward the house. He was still wearing his cutoffs and the open denim shirt.

"Be still my heart." Mom patted her chest and sighed, then winked at Jennie. "All right, I'm going. I promise I won't embarrass you. Just make sure blondie there keeps his distance."

Jennie rolled her eyes. "He's not my type," she muttered out of the corner of her mouth.

"Hi." Curtis trudged up the steps and sank into one of the padded wicker chairs. "Nice house."

"Thanks. Would you like a lemonade or something?"

"Yeah. Could I get a glass of water first, though, and maybe wash up and clean some of the bugs off my body? My windshield is being fixed, and I managed to pick up half the bugs in the county."

Though she tried not to look, her gaze drifted down to his bug-splattered chest. "I see what you mean." Trying not to laugh, Jennie led him to the bathroom. "You're welcome to take a shower." She handed him a towel and a bar of soap, then closed the door and barely made it to the kitchen before collapsing in a fit of giggles.

"What's so funny?" Mom set a couple glasses in the dishwasher and dried her hands.

Jennie held her stomach and gasped out the explanation.

Mom chuckled. "This is awful. We shouldn't be laughing at him."

"I know—but all those bugs . . ." She doubled over in another attack of laughter. By the time Curtis emerged from the bathroom, Jennie had managed to compose herself.

"Hey, thanks for the use of the shower." Curtis stood in the doorway of the kitchen and leaned against the doorjamb. His damp hair hung in ringlets and dripped water onto his broad shoulders.

"I hate to bother you, but I really could use a drink of water."

"Sure." Jennie handed him a glass, carried his lemonade out to the porch, and set the tray on the wicker table.

Jennie took the swing and Curtis lowered himself onto the chaise lounge and stretched his long, muscular legs out in front of him. After downing his ice water, he set the glass aside and tossed Jennie a lazy grin. "Did you get to see Gavin?"

"Yeah—only he didn't want to see me."

"I sort of figured that."

"Why? Did he tell you something about me?" Jennie set

the swing in motion and tucked one of her legs underneath her.

"Just off-the-wall stuff. He says you shot him."

"What?" Jennie bounced to her feet. "That ungrateful creep—I saved his life."

"Hey." Curtis raised his hands as if he expected her to hit him. "I didn't say I believed him."

"How could he say something like that?" Jennie backed up until the back of her knees hit the swing and fell back against the cushions. "I could understand when he was stoned out of his mind, but you'd think whatever he was on would have worn off by now."

"Some drugs are hallucinogenic. The effects can last for several days."

"Like LSD."

"Right. For the record, Jennie, I know you didn't do any of the stuff he's saying you did. That's why I wanted to talk to you. I might know who killed Dr. Mancini. But I need your help to prove it."

Jennie stilled the swing. "How did you know he was a doctor?"

Curtis shrugged. "He told me."

"Why come to me?" Jennie asked. "If you have information, you should be talking to the police."

"I told them, but they aren't interested. They're sure whoever killed Dr. Mancini was close to him—a friend or family member. Hey, they're even looking at Alex and Mrs. Mancini." He paused to take a drink.

"And you?"

"At first. Fortunately I have an alibi. I was working. My brother has this Harley dealership."

"What makes you think the police aren't interested in what you have to say? Did you talk to Lieutenant Rastovski?"

"Yeah. He thought my theory—and unfortunately that's all it is right now—sounded like a plot for a medical thriller.

Said they had enough viable suspects without chasing some fantasy."

Jennie leaned forward. "I like medical thrillers myself."

Curtis grinned. "I was hoping you'd say that. See, I think we should pool our resources. Maybe between the two of us, we can come up with enough evidence to convince the police they're on the wrong trail. There's just one problem, Jennie. We have to keep our investigation totally confidential. I mean you can't tell anybody what we're doing."

Jennie eyed him suspiciously. "Why?"

Curtis glanced around, then shifted over to the swing and lowered his voice. "The people involved in this project are extremely powerful. If they think for one minute we're on to them, they'll kill us."

"Sounds like you're talking about a drug cartel or the mob."

"They're worse, Jennie." His sky-blue eyes grayed with a mixture of concern and fear. "A lot worse."

# 17

Jennie could see why Lieutenant Rastovski might be skeptical—especially if Curtis had been as melodramatic with the police as he had been with her. If he hadn't seemed so sincere, she might have laughed at the idea herself. But Jennie figured it was just crazy enough to have some validity. And that frightened her.

Jennie shook her head to emphasize the point. "No way am I getting involved in anything that dangerous."

"It'll only be dangerous if the wrong people find out."

"Curtis—"

"Wait. Don't make up your mind yet. At least wait until I tell you what Dr. Mancini was working on."

Jennie pulled her long, thick braid from behind her back and wound it around her hand. "Okay. I'm listening, but do you think you could move back to the other chair?" For some strange reason, having Curtis sitting so close was stirring up the butterflies in her stomach.

He frowned. "Sure. Um—do I have bad breath or something?"

"No, nothing like that."

"So sitting close to me bothers you?" Curtis caught her gaze and held it. A knowing smile lifted the corners of his mouth. "Cool."

"Go." She shoved his shoulder when he scooted closer.

Still grinning, he plopped himself down on the chair closest to the swing. "I'm sorry, Jen. That was crude. Um—you're a really nice girl and—"

"Forget it. Just tell me about Mancini."

Suddenly serious again, Curtis raked both hands through his drying hair and pulled it back away from his face. "I'm not sure where to start."

"The beginning's always good. Like when did you meet him? And what's he like?"

"Right. Mancini came in as a sub right after Mr. Adams got sick. I knew right off there was something special about him."

"I heard a lot of kids didn't like him."

"That's putting it mildly. He expected a lot out of his students—too much. In fact, if it hadn't been for Michael, he'd probably have flunked half the class."

"What did Michael do?"

"Do you know Brian Stone? What am I saying? Everybody knows Brian. Anyway, Mancini failed Brian. Brian and his dad went in to talk to Michael and complained. It's a long story, but the school board had a little talk with Mancini, telling him to lower his standards and use a curve to grade the kids or risk losing his job.

"Mancini grumbled about it but complied. He passed everyone except Brian. Brian might have squeaked through too if he hadn't cheated on the final. When Mancini found out about it he banned Brian from the class—permanently."

"Do you think Brian killed Dr. Mancini? I know the sports business is big, but—"

"No—at least I'm pretty sure he didn't. I'm only telling you this to make a point. Mancini didn't act like a high school teacher, so I checked up on him."

"And you found out he's really a professor and that he lost his job at Berkeley because he was using and selling drugs."

"Who told you that?"

Jennie started to tell him but decided not to. "It doesn't matter."

He shrugged. "It isn't true. When Dr. Mancini was interviewing me for lab assistant, I asked him why he'd taken a job at Trinity. He told me there'd been a big misunderstanding at the university. Someone started the rumor about him making and selling designer drugs, and he was asked to resign. Well, he *was* working on drugs—a drug—to be exact, but it was for Dawson's—a big pharmaceutical company in the Midwest. Dr. Mancini had a grant to develop a medication that would counter addictive behavior."

Dawson—Jennie remembered having seen the name on the computer when Douglas and Rastovski were looking through his files. It was the one Douglas couldn't access. "Addictive behavior? Like drugs and alcohol?"

"And tobacco and food—everything."

"Oh, come on." Jennie stopped the swing.

"I know it sounds too good to be true. Maybe that's why the police didn't believe me. But this drug is for real, Jennie. I've been working with Dr. Mancini all summer. He was getting ready to do the final tests on it. Now he's dead. I know there's a connection."

"I'm sorry, Curtis, but I don't follow you. This *medication*—if there is such a thing—would be wonderful. Why would anyone want to stop it from coming out?"

"Think about what might happen if a drug like that hit the market, Jennie."

"I imagine it would sell like crazy, making Dr. Mancini and the Dawson Pharmaceuticals very wealthy." Jennie frowned. "Are you saying someone stole the formula?"

"Someone did steal the formula. It was on a disk he kept locked up in his desk. He also had a copy on his hard drive—they're both gone."

"And you told the police all this?"

"That's part of the reason they don't believe me. They asked me to show them the notes and stuff, but there was nothing in the computer to back me up. Everything is gone."

"Do you think the pharmaceutical company took the formula to avoid having to pay Mancini a share?"

"No. I think it was someone who stood to lose a lot of money if the drug ever became available to the general public. The person who murdered Dr. Mancini and took the formula wanted to make sure it never got out."

"You mean like the alcohol and tobacco industries, or drug dealers."

"That's exactly what I mean."

Strange as it seemed, Curtis's medical thriller fantasy was beginning to make perfect sense. "If that's the case, how could you ever pin down the killer? A drug like that could cost alcohol and tobacco industries billions, and the drug business—both legal and illegal. We're talking about thousands of suspects here. There's no way we could track down the killer. Maybe the local police aren't interested in your story, but I'll bet my—" Jennie caught herself. She'd almost said Dad. "Um—my grandfather is an FBI agent. And there's a DEA agent—Douglas—who's working on the case with Lieutenant Rastovski. Did you talk to him?"

Curtis propped his elbows on his knees and rested his head on his hands for a long moment, then looked up. "Yeah. Douglas seemed kind of interested at first, but when I couldn't substantiate my story, he wrote me off too."

Jennie didn't know how to respond. She had no answers. If Curtis was right, finding Mancini's killer would be like trying to catch a guppy in the ocean. She told Curtis as much.

"I know it sounds impossible and maybe I'm crazy for even trying—I was just hoping we could work together. At least tell me what you have. I know you've been investigating on your own."

Jennie laughed. "I'd hardly call it that. All I've done so

far is convince the police that Mancini didn't commit suicide. I've drawn up a partial list of suspects, but that's about it."

"How did you know it wasn't suicide?"

Jennie explained about the suicide note and how it had been written after she'd been in the lab. "What I saw was a—" She glanced up at Curtis.

"What?"

"Maybe that's what it was—Dr. Mancini's formula."

"Can you remember any of it? A title, words?"

"Some. I wrote it down on a piece of paper."

"Where is it? Can I see?"

"I can't remember. I had it in Dr. Mancini's office." She closed her eyes trying to remember what she'd done with her notes. "Sorry, I probably gave it to the lieutenant or Douglas."

"Can you remember what you saw?"

Jennie described what she'd seen. "It's not much, I know, but who knows? I may remember more later."

"Not that it will do much good. The formula is gone."

"You said you'd worked with Dr. Mancini. Don't you remember it?"

"Bits and pieces. He never let me see the entire work. Told me I was better off not knowing. Maybe he was right."

Curtis glanced up at the sky. The hazy blue had turned to battleship gray. Thunder rumbled in the distance. "I should go. I want to stop and see Gavin before I head home."

Jennie stood up when he did and walked him to the porch steps. "I'd have you tell him hi from me, but he'd probably freak out."

"He'll come out of it eventually. At least I hope so." The worried look in his eyes didn't offer much hope.

After he left, Jennie stuck a pillow against the arm of the swing and leaned against it, settling her legs on the seat. The darkening crimson sky began to deliver on its promise of rain. *Angel's teardrops*, Dad had told her once. Jennie smiled at the distant memory. If that was the case, all the angels in heaven were terribly sad at the moment.

Curtis would be drenched by the time he reached the hospital—but at least he wouldn't be covered with bugs. She chuckled softly. Though she found Curtis attractive—who wouldn't—she'd never date him. She could see it now. He'd put his arm around her, they'd close their eyes, and he'd lower his head and press his lips against hers. Then she'd remember the bugs and shatter the romantic mood by laughing herself into hysterics.

*Besides,* she reminded herself, *you aren't really interested in Curtis Bolton—you have Ryan Johnson. And in a few days you'll be able to see him.*

Still, she found Curtis a definite curiosity. He'd changed physically, but there were other changes too. Like the motorcycle, and maybe even his personality. She hadn't known Curtis that well but remembered him as being more of a nerd—studious, withdrawn, and shy. Now he seemed more self-assured—a little on the wild side. Jennie shrugged. Maybe he was just going through a phase—trying to find himself. At least that's what Mom would say.

She shifted her attention from Curtis to the professor. So, Dr. Mancini had been working for a pharmaceutical company—just like Gram had said. Interesting. Maybe that's where Mrs. Mancini and Alex got the money for their trip to Europe. If that was the case, it didn't seem likely they'd have killed him for a life insurance policy. He'd have been worth much more alive and stood to make millions if the drug was ever approved by the FDA.

Mancini had been forced to leave Berkeley after a rumor of drug use. Jennie found that especially believable since someone was trying to set her up as well. Coincidence? She doubted it. Had someone followed him to Portland—which brought up another question. How had he ended up at Trinity? It seemed an odd transition. Maybe she'd ask Michael about it tomorrow—after Dr. Mancini's funeral. She'd have another talk with Rastovski too and maybe Douglas. It seemed strange that they'd ignore Curtis's theory altogether. Maybe they hadn't. Jennie had a feeling Rastovski was one of those guys who didn't miss a beat.

The light drizzle turned into a deluge, and Jennie set her questions and plans on hold. For the moment, she wanted to close out anything to do with the murder and concentrate on the spectacular summer storm.

Jennie breathed deeply, relishing the musty sweet smell of wet earth and grass. She closed her eyes and listened as the rain pattered against the roof above her and rattled through the downspout on the side of the house.

The door opened and a board creaked as Mom came out to join her. "Hi. Thought you might be getting cold." Mom covered her with a patchwork quilt of purple, pink, and teal.

Jennie sat up and snuggled under it, just now aware of the goose bumps on her arms and legs. "Thanks. Want to watch the storm with me?"

"Wouldn't miss it."

Jennie shifted around so her mother could share the quilt.

The downpour continued for about ten minutes, then let up as the light show began in earnest. Thunder rolled and crashed with the fury of waves against the rocks at high tide. The streetlights sputtered and died. For brief spine-chilling moments, lightning turned the night to day. Their excitement grew as the storm moved over them. Between clashes of thunder Jennie thought she could hear the sound of a motorcycle and wondered briefly if Curtis had decided to come back.

A clap of thunder shook the house, and the sky around them flashed white. Mother and daughter ducked in unison. The action tipped them out of the swing and dumped them on the porch.

Jennie started to get up. Another sharp crack, then another, made her duck again. Something whizzed past her head and slammed into the wood above their heads. *Thunk. Thunk.*

"What in the world—?" Mom raised up on her knees to look at the splintered wood.

"Stay down." Jennie reached for her mother and sprawled behind the porch railing. "Stay down," she gasped again. "Someone's shooting at us!"

# 18

Thunder exploded around them again, nearly obliterating the screech of tires and the distinctive sound of a motorcycle speeding away.

Silence stretched for an eternity. Jennie's heart slammed against her chest so hard she felt certain she was putting dents in the floor beneath her.

"I think he's gone," Mom whispered.

"I hope so." Jennie lifted her head and peered between the posts on the railing. The streetlights flickered on, then off, then on again.

"I'll crawl into the house and call the police." Mom began moving toward the door.

"Wait." Jennie grabbed an ankle. "It might be safer if we go around back."

They crawled along the side porch. When they reached the rear of the house, they sprinted over the grass and in the back door.

Mom dove for the phone and called 9–1–1.

Jennie huddled under the quilt she'd dragged in with her from the porch. She hadn't realized she'd brought it until that moment. A shiver ran through her and she pulled the quilt tighter. Jennie thought about turning on the light, then decided against it. They hadn't drawn the shades, and the light would make them clear targets if the gunman was still around. The streetlamp provided enough light for the moment.

When her knees threatened to give way, Jennie shuffled to the kitchen table and dropped into a chair.

Mom hung up the phone after talking to the 9–1–1 operator. "Someone will be out in a few minutes. I suppose I should turn on the porch light." Instead of going to the front door Mom grasped Jennie's shoulders and began massaging them.

That's how Lieutenant Rastovski found them. He hadn't bothered to knock—just barged in. He snapped on the kitchen light and stared from Mom to Jennie, then back to Mom again. Maybe he thought they'd been killed or something, because he sure looked relieved when he saw them.

Mom's fingers dug into Jennie's shoulders.

"I was on my way home when the call came in." He cleared his throat.

The tension between them was like a magnetic force so strong Jennie felt certain that any second now they'd end up in each other's arms.

Rastovski looked away. "I take it I'm the first officer to arrive?"

"I only called a few minutes ago." Mom released Jennie's shoulders, walked over to the cupboard, and retrieved two cups. "Would you like some coffee?"

Mom was in shock, Jennie realized. Maybe they all were.

The lieutenant shook his head. "Just tell me what happened."

"Jennie and I were sitting on the porch watching the thunderstorm when someone shot at us."

"Did you see anything?"

"No," Jennie answered this time. "It was too dark. But I heard something, a motorcycle." She told him about Curtis Bolton's visit. "He said he was going to the hospital, but he may have decided to come back and shoot me instead."

"Why would he do that? You two have an argument?"

"No." Jennie wished she'd kept her mouth shut. "It probably wasn't him—it's just that I thought I heard a motorcycle and wondered if he'd come back. After the shooting, I heard the motorcycle take off again."

"Show me where it happened."

Mom led the way to the porch and Jennie followed. They were pointing out the bullet holes and wood splinters when a squad car pulled up to the curb—lights flashing. Another car screeched in behind, then another.

"Stay here," Rastovski ordered, then descended the steps to meet the officers. "What took you so long?"

"Got here as fast as we could. A lot going down tonight." The officer hitched up his belt. "What have we got?"

"Looks like a drive-by. Not sure about motive. No injuries. We're looking for a biker. Check on the whereabouts of a Curtis Bolton. Young kid, long blond hair. He was supposed to be visiting a friend—Gavin Winslow over at Sunnyside. See if he made it. If not, find him."

They talked for a few minutes, then two officers went to their cars while a third retrieved a roll of yellow tape from his trunk and began taping off their porch.

Rastovski returned to where Jennie and Mom were standing and herded them back into the house. "We'll have a team of officers out here for a while, gathering evidence," he told them. "Appreciate it if you could stay inside."

"Lieutenant?" Jennie stopped in the entry and turned around. "Can you match a bike's tires to the skid marks on the pavement?"

"Sometimes. Why?"

"Well, when Curtis came, he squealed around the corner." She pointed toward Magnolia and Elm. "Whoever shot at us burned rubber when he accelerated. He was heading back around the same corner."

"Thanks, Jennie. We'll check it out." His dark gaze

caught hers in an affirming gesture.

Maybe Rastovski wasn't such a bad guy after all.

"Isn't there something I could do to help?" Mom asked. "I feel so restless and—it's not every day one gets shot at."

"Maybe you could bake something."

Mom tipped her head and gave him an odd look. "Brownies?"

"Sounds good to me." Rastovski looked like he was about to pull Mom into his arms and kiss her.

*He's a cop, Mom*, Jennie wanted to shout in warning. *You don't like cops, remember?* "I'll be in my room," she announced instead, then trounced up the stairs and didn't look back.

Shutting her bedroom door did nothing to close out the vision of Rastovski and Mom. The more Jennie saw the two of them together, the more puzzled she became. Mom was falling for this guy, hard and fast, which wasn't like Mom at all. After Dad had disappeared, she waited almost five years before even starting to date again. With Michael, things had progressed slowly. Mom had seemed sure for a while, then backed off. She'd seen Rastovski two, maybe three times, and she was acting more in love than she ever had with Michael.

Jennie wandered over to her dresser and picked up Dad's picture. His dark blue eyes smiled up at her. "Oh, Dad. What are we going to do? Please come home before it's too late. The way she looks at Lieutenant Rastovski would break your heart." Tears gathered in her eyes and dripped onto the glass. She gathered the photo to her chest and hugged it, then curled up in her window seat.

After a while, the sobbing stopped. It did no good at all to cry. Life was getting too complicated, but that didn't mean she had to give up. She set Dad's photo back and padded to the phone. After dialing, she fell back onto the bed.

"Hello?"

Just hearing Gram's voice settled Jennie's frazzled nerves. "Hi, Gram. It's me."

"Jennie! I'm so glad you called. J.B. and I were watching the news. They reported a drive-by shooting in your area but didn't released any names. We were worried."

"It was here. They were shooting at Mom and me."

"Oh, my goodness! Are you all right?"

"We're fine. The police are here." Jennie went on to explain what had happened.

"Was Nick there too? That poor darling—"

"No. He's staying over at Kate's tonight."

"How is your mother taking it? I imagine she's terrified."

"Actually, she's doing pretty well. She's baking brownies for Lieutenant Rastovski."

"Really?"

"Gram, she just made a batch on Monday. I think she's losing it." Jennie filled her in on that complication as well and ended by telling about having been arrested that morning.

"My, you have had a busy day. Hold on a moment, darling. I need to talk to J.B."

Jennie could hear Gram giving J.B. the condensed version of what had been going on. "We'll be there around ten tomorrow morning, Jennie. Has your mother called Kate?"

"No."

"I'll call her. We need to let her know before she hears it on the news. I don't understand why Susan didn't call."

"She's pretty upset—and with Rastovski hanging around—I don't know, Gram. You need to have a talk with her."

"It can't be that bad."

"It is. I'm afraid she's falling for this guy and—we need to tell her about Dad before she gets too involved. Um—did you find out any more?"

"I'm afraid not, dear. J.B. says your father's superiors have taken the matter under consideration, but they're not divulging any information."

"Not even to you and J.B.?"

"No. J.B. thinks they may have him hooked into a big case, so it may be a while. At any rate, I don't think you need to worry. Your mother is one of the most level-headed women I know. She's not going to rush in to anything—especially a wedding."

"I hope not."

"Jennie, one more thing. I don't feel comfortable having you and your mother in the house alone tonight. You should go over to Kate's."

Jennie agreed and after hanging up released a long, low whistle. Gram and J.B. were coming back. Feeling ten times better, Jennie headed downstairs to check on Mom and to let her know they had company coming.

Jennie followed the decadent scent of dark fudge brownies into the kitchen. They were cooling on a rack near the stove. Jennie licked her lips and retrieved a knife. After cutting out a one-inch square she popped it into her mouth. "Hmm."

Susan McGrady gave her daughter a cursory glance, then went back to unloading the dishwasher. "He's quite something, isn't he?" Mom said before Jennie had a chance to give her the good news.

"Who?"

"The lieutenant."

Jennie shrugged. "Something as in bossy and arrogant—"

Mom closed the dishwasher. "He reminds me of your father in some ways—only he's more attentive—more considerate."

"Oh, please. He's nothing like Dad. He's mean-tempered, and he actually thinks I might be a murderer. Dad would never think that."

"Hmm," Mom went on as if Jennie hadn't said a word. "He even has some of the same mannerisms." Mom pulled the teakettle from the burner when it began whistling. "Would you like some tea?"

Jennie stared at her. "If Rastovski reminds you of Dad, why do you like him so much?"

Now it was Mom's turn to stare. "I loved your father, Jennie. We didn't agree on a lot of things, but . . ." She shook her head as if coming out of a trance, then poured water into two cups, dunking a tea bag in one, then the other.

"I called Gram," Jennie announced. "She and J.B. are coming back tomorrow. Did you call Aunt Kate?"

"No—I—" Mom brushed her hand across her forehead and frowned. "I suppose I should"—she glanced at her watch—"they're probably still up."

"Don't worry about it. Gram's calling her."

Mom sighed and brought the steaming cups to the table. "I don't know what's gotten into me lately. I hope Gram isn't upset with me."

"Mom, it's okay. I took care of it."

Mom pulled out a chair and lowered herself into it. "You said they'd be down tomorrow?"

"Uh-huh. Gram said we should go over to Kate's tonight. We'll be safer there."

Mom shook her head. "It's too late. I don't think that's necessary."

The doorbell rang. Jennie jumped up. "I'll get it. Just drink your tea." Mom looked pale and shaky—and tired.

Rastovski walked in before Jennie could get to the door. "Where's your mother?" He headed toward the kitchen without waiting for an answer.

"Did you find out anything?" Jennie followed him down the hall into the kitchen.

He didn't respond. Instead he stopped next to the table and tugged at his tie. "I want you two out of the house tonight. You got someplace you can stay? If not, I'll put you up in a hotel."

Mom shook her head. "I'm not leaving. I absolutely refuse to be chased out of my own home by some hoodlum."

"Susan—"

"No. Jennie can go stay with Kate—my sister-in-law. In fact, that's probably not a bad idea, but I'm staying."

"Mom, he's right. We should go—Gram even said so."

Mom shook her head.

"Are you always this stubborn?"

"Only when it matters."

"And this matters."

"Yes—yes it does."

"Fine," Rastovski pulled out a chair and sat down. "You stay, then I'll stay. I can sleep on the couch."

"There's no need—"

"Yes, there is. This wasn't a random drive-by. I had an officer check out the lead Jennie gave us on the Bolton kid. She was right. He never showed up at the hospital."

# 19

Rastovski must have read the shock on Jennie's face. "Why are you so surprised—you're the one who put us on to him."

"I just didn't think—I mean—I only mentioned him because of the motorcycle. I didn't really believe he'd try to shoot me."

"We don't know for sure, of course, but we put out an APB on him. If he's out there, we'll find him. In the meantime, I want you two in a safe place."

"You think he'll come back?" Mom asked.

"My guess is he was after Jennie. He either wanted to scare her or kill her. If it's the first, we probably don't have to worry about him showing up again. If it's the latter, he missed and will probably try again. The police chief isn't willing to put out the money for an officer to stand guard all night, so that leaves two options. Either you and Jennie go somewhere safe, or I stay here."

When Mom stood up, Rastovski straightened and eyed her wearily.

"Would you like some coffee to go with your brownies?" She turned away from him and headed for the counter.

"Please." He fastened a dark, wistful gaze on Mom before turning to Jennie. "Tell me everything you know about this Bolton kid."

"That wouldn't be much. I've known him from school since sixth grade, but we were never friends. He and Gavin hung out together. I didn't know that until today."

"Why was he here? You two have a date or something?"

"No. He was at the hospital when Mom and I went to see Gavin. He said he wanted to talk to me. Told me about an anti-addiction drug Dr. Mancini was working on."

Rastovski leaned back when Mom returned with his brownie and a cup of coffee. "Anything else?"

"He seemed to think someone had framed Dr. Mancini at Berkeley in order to keep the drug from being manufactured and that someone may have killed him and stolen the formula." She reiterated Curtis's theory.

"He told us the same story, but why would he tell you?"

"Because you didn't believe him and he thought maybe I could help him solve the case."

"Then he comes back and tries to gun you down? I don't think so." He picked up his fork and cut off a sizeable chunk of the rich dessert, then dipped it into the whipped topping Mom had placed on top. "He didn't want your help in solving the case, Jennie. He wanted information. What did you tell him?"

"Just that I saw something on the computer screen that might have been Dr. Mancini's formula. I told him what I remembered about it. Which reminds me. Did you take the paper I wrote part of the formula on when we were in Dr. Mancini's office?"

"Agent Douglas is checking it out."

Mom placed two more desserts on the table, then sat down. "Lieutenant, doesn't it seem rather strange to you that we now have three kids—probably three of the top students at Trinity High—who have suddenly turned criminal?"

Rastovski chased his bite with a swig of coffee. "I'm not sure I follow you."

"Well, first Gavin Winslow turns up missing. He's obviously been given drugs and somehow brainwashed to believe Jennie was involved in abducting him and dealing drugs. Then someone, possibly Gavin, plants drugs in Jennie's car and turns her in. She's arrested, taking her out of circulation. Since that apparently didn't stop her, they try to gun her— or us—down. Now Curtis is being sought in a drive-by shooting."

"Your point?" Rastovski's annoyed tone didn't match the twinkle in his eyes. He seemed amused and disgruntled at the same time. It was almost as though he liked the idea that Mom would have an opinion on the case.

"These kids have several things in common," Mom continued. "They are all top students, they all go to Trinity High, and they have all been trying to make sense of their teacher's murder."

When Mom paused to eat a bite of her brownie, Jennie took up the slack. "Mom has a good point. Someone has been trying to discredit—or maybe even get rid of—Gavin and me, just like they did Dr. Mancini at Berkeley. Maybe Curtis is being set up too."

"So you're thinking Bolton's conspiracy theory has merit?" Rastovski directed his question at Mom.

"It makes perfect sense to me. Gavin called Jennie just before he disappeared saying he had a major breakthrough in the case. Jennie interrupted the killer and saw something on that computer screen that could have been an important piece of evidence. And Curtis? If what he told Jennie about working with Dr. Mancini on this miracle drug is true, he may be able to reproduce it."

Jennie glanced at Rastovski, who seemed to be seriously considering Mom's ideas. "So, if Bolton is right in thinking someone wants to keep the drug off the market, that would make him a threat too."

"Exactly."

Rastovski popped the last piece of brownie in his mouth,

looking thoughtful as he chewed. "We got a lot of *if*s here. I agree, there may be some merit to Bolton's story, but I'm not sure I buy this idea of Mancini developing a drug that's going to make addictions a thing of the past. Too far fetched. Still, the DEA is working that angle. Douglas is more inclined to think Mancini was using the lab at Trinity to produce designer drugs. Either Bolton was working with him, or the professor was stringing him along with the story about the antiaddiction pill."

"Designer drugs?" Mom stroked the rim of her cup. "I've heard that term before, but I'm not sure what it means."

"It's a term we give certain look-alike drugs. They contain over-the-counter ingredients and resemble various prescription or illegal dugs." For the next ten minutes Rastovski lectured them about the availability of drugs and how the DEA and other law-enforcement agencies barely made a dent in the street availability of narcotics.

Despite her fascination with Rastovski's explanations, Jennie's eyes kept closing and her brain seemed bent on shutting down for the night. She folded her arms on the table and rested her head. *Just for a minute*, she told herself. *I'll just close my eyes for a minute.*

"Jennie? Come on, sweetheart, wake up. Better get to bed." Mom squeezed Jennie's shoulders. "I'll be up as soon as I clear the table."

Jennie obeyed the voice and didn't resist the strong, masculine arms that helped her to her feet and half carried her out of the kitchen and up the stairs.

"Come on, princess," a tender baritone voice whispered in her ear. "Just a few more steps."

Still more than half asleep, Jennie stumbled into her room and turned on the lamp beside her bed. After saying goodnight to the closing door, she tossed aside the decorative pillows and turned down the covers. She thought briefly of getting up and changing into her pajamas, but that would require a hundred times more energy than she had at the moment. She barely had the strength to reach up and turn off the light.

Stretching out on the bed, Jennie glanced at the red numbers on her digital clock. Twelve-thirty. Why wasn't she falling asleep? Something important scratched at the back of her mind like a dog wanting to be let in. She closed her eyes tight, but the harder she tried to sleep, the more restless she became.

The room was too light. She'd forgotten to close the blinds. The storm had passed and the moon beamed in almost enough light to read by. Jennie groaned and got up. After closing the blinds, she padded to her closet and flipped on the light.

Then it hit her. Rastovski had burst into the house only minutes after the shooting and hit the light switch in the kitchen like he was familiar with the place. He'd called her princess.

Jennie gasped for air, her closet suddenly too small and cramped for the emotions exploding around and through her. She ran to her dresser, grabbed Dad's picture, and turned on the bedside lamp. Dropping onto the bed, she studied the familiar face in the photo.

It couldn't be him. He looked so different, yet there were similarities as well. When she'd first met Rastovski he'd looked familiar to her. She thought he reminded her of her cousin, Hazen, with his dark hair and eyes. The McGradys had dark features as well.

*You are so dense, McGrady. You should have seen it right away.* Of course, the last time she'd seen Dad, he'd lightened his hair—and had a receding hairline. She hadn't recognized him right away then either. His eyes had finally given him away. Rastovski's eyes were the color of dark chocolate. And the scar on his face—a recent injury? His voice was different too—harsher, raspier—except for when he'd called her princess.

She examined the photo again and tried to superimpose the features of the man. It couldn't be. Yet—maybe it could. Rastovski was new to the area—Rocky had told her that.

"What happened, Dad? Are you Nate Rastovski? If so, why are you here? Have you told Mom?" Jennie didn't think so. Mom would have said something. Wouldn't she?

Jennie set the photo down and headed for the door. What was the point in asking herself all those questions when her father was downstairs?

No way would she be able to sleep now. She tiptoed into the dark hallway. Two doors down a light leaked out of Mom's bedroom onto the taupe carpet. Good, Mom was probably in bed.

Jennie crept downstairs and paused before going into the living room—partly to let her eyes adjust to the darkness and partly to muster up enough courage to confront Rastovski. *What if you're wrong, McGrady? Dad is a DEA agent, not a homicide investigator.*

*Yes, but Rastovski knows an awful lot about drugs. Maybe he changed jobs.*

*He'd never do that,* Jennie argued against her own logic. *And Dad would never have discussed a case with her and Mom like Rastovski had.*

But he had called her princess. She had to know.

"Thought you were asleep." Rastovski's husky voice shattered the silence and her thoughts. He adjusted the pillows on the couch and sat down.

"I was—almost—only now I can't sleep." Jennie sank down beside him.

"Join the club."

"Why didn't you tell me?"

The momentary silence as he removed his shoes gave her the assurance she needed. This man was definitely her father.

"Tell you what?"

"Who you really are."

He hesitated again.

"You called me princess." Jennie's eyes had adjusted to the semidarkness, but she still couldn't make out his features.

He sighed. "I was hoping you hadn't noticed. I should have known better."

"You knew where the light switch was in the kitchen—and you still like brownies."

"Your mother had me going for a while with that. I thought maybe she'd figured it out."

"You haven't told her?"

"Not yet. To be honest, I hadn't expected our paths to cross quite so soon. I was hoping to get settled in my job and get some loose ends tied up. I will tell her, though. I just haven't found the right time. Guess I wanted to see if there was a possibility of us getting together."

"Of course there is. She likes you a lot."

"You really think so?"

"Yeah." Jennie glanced at him—part of her wanted to throw her arms around his neck—part of her wanted to strangle him. "Are you staying?"

"If I can. If your mother will take me back."

"What about your job with the DEA?"

"I haven't worked for the DEA in weeks. After you met me in the Caribbean, I went on to Jamaica. Major cartel there. We set up a sting operation, but someone set us up. Five of us walked into a trap—three agents were killed. Douglas and I made it out, but we both ended up in a hospital in Florida. He took a bullet in the shoulder. I was there for about three weeks, getting myself sewn back together." He reached up and touched the scar on his face.

"Why didn't you let me know? I could have come to see you."

"I couldn't at that time."

164

"Too dangerous?"

"That and other things. Anyway, being laid up gave me a lot of time to think about my life—about what really mattered. Got to talking to God a lot and praying. I realized I made a big mistake years ago by placing my career so far ahead of my family. Thought I was making the big sacrifice. Noble as my goals were, I made some choices I deeply regret. I just hope you and Susan and Nick can forgive me. There's nothing I can do about the past. But I *can* do something about the present. Things have changed, princess. I've changed. I want to come home. Be with my wife and kids. I just hope it isn't too late."

"Oh, Dad." Jennie touched his arm. "It's never too late. But promise me you'll tell Mom right away. It's been awful trying to keep secrets from her. I prayed every night that you'd come back before she married Michael. Now you're here."

"She's going to be furious when she learns how the government—how we lied to her—letting her believe I was dead."

"She'll get over it." *I hope.* "Besides, you did it to protect us. She'll understand."

Dad slipped an arm around her shoulder. "It feels so good to be home—I'm glad you figured it out."

"I'm glad you finally got here." Jennie sighed. "There's just one problem."

"What's that?"

"Why did you have to come back as Nate Rastovski? The guy's a total jerk."

Jennie bounced off the sofa before he could swat her. She came around behind him and wrapped her arms around his neck. "Good night, Dad."

"Good night, Jennie."

Jennie paused when she got to the stairs, then spun around and joined her father on the couch. "I know it's late, but there's something I gotta know."

"What's that?"

"Are you for real working with the Portland police on this Mancini case?"

"Yeah, and a number of others."

"How come you were so ready to call it a suicide? Did you really think it was?"

"It would have been so much easier if it had been." He smiled. "But no. As soon as I read the crime scene analysis and autopsy report I knew."

Jennie lifted her hair into a tail and pulled it foward. "So you really didn't need me to tell you."

"I think I'd have eventually figured it out, yes. But I really did appreciate your insight."

"What was it like? Seeing a dead body, I mean. I keep imagining what it must have looked like—pretty messy, huh?"

"No, not really." Rastovski stretched his long legs out in front of him and crossed them at the ankle. "That's one of the things that threw us at first. It looked as though Mancini had wrapped a towel around his head before he shot himself. One way of keeping his lab clean—it was consistent with his penchant for neatness. It also made it more difficult for us to determine exactly what happened. Most of the time we can pretty much look at the blood spatters and determine what went down."

"So how did the medical examiner figure out it wasn't a suicide?"

"Two things. There was a bump and cut on the back of his head. At first we figured he must have bumped it when he fell after the shooting. Only that wasn't consistent with what we found. The medical examiner says he had to have hit his head on the counter before wrapping his head in a towel and shooting himself, only that couldn't have happened because the first head wound killed him."

"Wow. So he was already dead when someone shot him." Jennie was getting more excited by the second—imagine, discussing a murder with her own father.

"Right."

"You said there were two things that tipped you off. What was the other?"

"The crank he was supposed to have taken was injected after he'd already died."

Jennie bit her lower lip. She had a feeling she knew what he'd say, but had to ask anyway. "I still think you should use me as bait to flush out the killer."

"Absolutely not. I wouldn't let any kid do that, Jennie, especially not my daughter. Like I said before, Douglas and I will take care of it. We have a number of leads."

"Speaking of which—did you really consider me a suspect?"

"Of course not."

"Then why did you have me arrested?"

"I had to treat you like I would anyone else under those circumstances."

"I suppose I shouldn't ask you to fix a ticket for me then."

He chuckled. "What do you think?"

Jennie shrugged her shoulders. "Yes?"

"Go to bed, Jennie. We'll have lots of time to talk later, but right now we both need some rest."

Jennie moaned. "Maybe I could stay down here with you. I could sleep on the floor—"

"I don't think so, Jennie."

"Okay, okay. I'm going." She hugged him again, then one more time for good measure and reluctantly climbed back up the stairs.

As pumped as she was, Jennie had no trouble falling asleep. Staying that way proved more difficult. She'd heard a car door slam at five-thirty. The phone rang at six. Jennie cuddled the receiver to her ear. "H'lo."

"Jennie—this is Gavin. Get over here right away."

"Where are you?"

"At the hospital—I have to talk to you."

"But I thought—"

"Look, I'm sorry, okay?"

"No, it's not okay—you caused me a lot of trouble—"

"Just get here as soon as you can. We don't have much time."

# 20

Jennie hung up and pulled the covers over her head. "I'm not going," she muttered into her pillow.

*Come on, McGrady, get up. You have to go.*

The phone rang again. She thought about ignoring it but reached for the receiver anyway.

"I'm sorry I hung up on you."

"What do you want, Gavin?"

"Please come. I am so scared. They got Curtis and we're going to be next."

"What are you talking about?"

"Curtis was supposed to come by the hospital last night—only he didn't. The cops came instead. They think he shot at you, but he didn't—someone is setting him up."

"This isn't making any sense."

"Look, Jen—it's a long story. I—I can't talk now." He hung up again.

Jennie heaved an exasperated sigh and climbed out of bed. Raising the blinds, she noticed Rastovski's—Dad's—car was still parked in the driveway. Douglas's green Honda stood behind it. He was probably downstairs going over the details of the case with Dad. *Dad.* Wow, the thought of having her father home sent her spirits flying.

The sun was just coming up, promising a clear day. The scent of bacon wafted up through the floor vents and made her stomach growl.

Jennie showered and dressed quickly in her jeans and a T-shirt—the royal blue one with a Dancing Waters Dude Ranch logo on the pocket. Wearing it again made her long for the mountains and the cousins, aunt, and uncle she'd left behind. She had to remember to write them another letter—as soon as this nightmare with Mancini and her own arrest were over. She had no doubt it would be over soon with Dad working on the case. Maybe he'd even fix her parking ticket.

Downstairs in the kitchen, Mom, Rastovski, and Douglas were talking in hushed tones over bacon, eggs, hashbrowns, toast, and grapefruit halves. And of course, coffee.

They stopped talking when she came in. "My, you're up early," Mom said. "Hope we didn't wake you."

"No." Jennie kissed her mother on the cheek and moved toward Dad, then froze when she realized what she'd almost done. She was going to have to be extremely careful—at least until Dad let Mom know the truth. "Hi, guys," she patted her father's shoulder. "Catch the creep who shot at us yet?"

"No." Douglas scowled. "But we will."

Mom started to get up, but Jennie stopped her. "I'll get my own." She popped a slice of sourdough bread in the toaster and dished up a couple of eggs. While she waited for the toast, she poured a glass of milk. "Um—Mom, do you mind if I go to the hospital this morning to see how Gavin is doing?"

"Are you sure you want to? After yesterday—"

"He called me this morning and wants to see me. I think whatever he was on must have worn off, 'cause he sounded more like his old self."

"That is good news." She glanced at her watch. "I guess it would be okay. You could stop at Kate and Kevin's and pick up Nick and Bernie for me on your way home—save me a trip. I have got to get some filing done today. My office is starting to look like a storage room."

"I don't like it." Dad's scowl matched his friend's. These

guys were obviously in a foul mood. "You shouldn't be going out by yourself."

The toast popped up, and Jennie's heart jumped with it. He wasn't going to let her go.

"I could take her," Douglas said. "I need to question the Winslow kid again anyway."

"That's great. Thanks." Jennie set her breakfast on the table and returned to the counter to get her milk. "After we see Gavin, you could drop me off at Kate's, and Lisa could bring Nick and me home later." She glanced at Mom. "That way you'd have more time to work."

Dad seemed pleased with the arrangement and excused himself, saying he had to get to work. "I'd like to come by later," he told Mom. "See how things are going. Be sure to keep the doors locked. I'll alert the officers assigned to this area to keep an eye on the house."

"I appreciate your concern, Lieutenant, but I'm sure I'll be fine." Mom gathered up empty plates and took them to the sink.

"Hate to break up the party, Mrs. McGrady, but I need to make a few phone calls." Douglas stood up and picked up the cell phone lying on the table. "Thanks for breakfast. I'll be out in my car when you're ready, Jennie."

Dad waited until Douglas was gone, then pushed his chair back. "I'd better be going too."

Mom tossed the dishcloth in the sink. "I'll walk you to the door."

Jennie wished she could tag along—be a fly on the wall and watch her parents say goodbye. Would he kiss her? Would he choose that moment to tell her? No, probably not—he needed a romantic dinner with candlelight and roses for that. Maybe she'd arrange something for that evening.

Before tackling her meal, Jennie asked a blessing. *Oh, and God, thanks for bringing Dad back. Open Mom's heart. Please don't let her be mad when she finds out.* She opened her eyes and picked up her fork.

"It'll work out," she murmured, trying to erase the uneasy feeling in the pit of her stomach. "It just has to."

Ten minutes later, Jennie grabbed her leather bag, kissed her mom goodbye, and ran out to the car. Douglas straightened, took a last drag of his cigarette, dropped it on the concrete, then ground it out with his shoe.

Jennie bristled but didn't say anything. Some people who smoked had the most disgusting habits—like blowing smoke in people's faces and tossing the butts on the ground. She was beginning to have second thoughts about riding with Douglas if she had to breathe in his secondhand smoke. But she did need to get to the hospital.

His car smelled of stale tobacco and, from the looks of the Burger King bag stuffed between the seats, yesterday's lunch.

Besides that, Jennie wasn't sure how things would work out with Douglas going with her to the hospital. Would he give her time alone with Gavin?

"Thanks for taking me." Jennie buckled her seat belt and tossed Douglas a smile she hoped looked sincere.

"No problem."

Douglas called in to the dispatch operator and told her he was on his way to Sunnyside, then tucked the receiver back on the radio. He wasn't much of a talker, and after several minutes of listening to the garbled message on the radio, Jennie felt like an overinflated balloon.

"S-so," she said, letting the word hiss through her teeth. "How long have you worked for the DEA?"

"About ten years." He glanced behind him and pulled into the right-hand lane.

"Bet you've cracked a lot of drug cases."

"Yep. Your dad and I have been through a lot together."

"How—?"

"He told me this morning. You're a clever girl, Jennie. Jason didn't think anyone would recognize him after his surgery."

"I guess there are some things a person can't erase."

"I suppose that's true."

"Have you changed your identity too? Do you have a family?"

"No on both counts."

"Um—Dad said you thought Dr. Mancini was making drugs in the lab at Trinity. Is that possible? I've heard about drug labs, but I thought they smelled really bad. Someone would have noticed."

"Not necessarily. Depends on what drugs are being manufactured and how they're processed. You're probably thinking of meth labs. Those will often have a strong odor—similar to cat urine."

"Curtis says Dr. Mancini was developing an anti-addiction drug."

He snorted. "So I hear."

"It should be pretty easy to find out—I mean, all you'd have to do is contact Dawson Pharmaceuticals."

"And you think we haven't done that?"

Jennie pinched her lips together. Great, now she'd offended him. Maybe she should just keep her mouth shut. "I'm sorry. I didn't mean to imply you weren't doing your job. I'm just curious—that's all."

"Don't worry. We're on top of it." Douglas exited the freeway and made a left on Sunnyside Road. He dropped her off in front of the hospital and said he'd meet her later in Gavin's room. Good, she'd have a chance to talk to Gavin alone—at least for as long as it took him to find a place to park. From the looks of the full parking lot, that could take a while.

"It's about time you got here," Gavin growled as she entered the room.

"You're lucky I got here at all. Now, what's so important

you had to get me out of bed at six in the morning?"

"Your life, for one thing." He glanced toward the open door.

Jennie pushed it shut, then picked up a chair on her way back to the bed. "Okay, what's up? You can start by telling me why you told the police I was a drug dealer." She dropped into the chair and propped one foot on the bed rail.

"I had no choice. They threatened to kill you and my parents if I didn't."

Jennie straightened and leaned forward. "Who're they?"

"I don't know."

"I'm not buying it, Gavin. Why didn't you just tell the police about the threats?"

"Oh, yeah, right. You know what they'd do. Nothing. I figured you'd be safer in jail. I knew you'd get off eventually."

"Thanks." Jennie folded her arms and leaned back. "Where does Curtis figure into all of this?"

"I'm not sure. All I know is he didn't shoot at you. And he doesn't do drugs."

"Are you sure about that? He's changed."

"Not really." Gavin used his trapeze to scoot up in bed.

"He showed up at my house on a motorcycle."

"His older brother has a dealership and gave Curtis a Harley for his birthday a few months ago."

"That's what Curtis told me. Whoever shot at me was riding a bike."

"Well, it couldn't have been Curtis."

"How can you be so sure?"

"Curtis would never get involved in anything like that. I know this guy, Jen."

Jennie sighed. "Okay, let's say he didn't shoot at me and he isn't into drugs. You said his brother sells bikes—could he be involved?"

"Hardly. Ray is the executive type."

"With a Harley dealership?"

"Yeah—he also owns a couple other companies."

"What about Brian Stone? Does he ride a motorcycle?"

"Brian? I have no idea. What does he have to do with anything?"

"Never mind. Just tell me what happened to you and we'll go from there."

"I'll try. All I know is that I got a call at the paper that day after you dropped me off—right after Mancini was killed. Curtis wanted me to meet him at Trinity. When I got there, he used his key to let us in the office."

"His key or Mancini's?"

"I don't know—he's the lab assistant, so I figured he'd have a key."

"But it was taped off—you weren't supposed to—"

"I know. It's just that Curtis was so torn up about the whole thing. He went on and on about how Mancini was such a nice guy and didn't deserve to die that way. He told me about the drug Mancini had developed and that now they'd be after him because he knew too much." Gavin recanted the same story Curtis had told her.

"I think he was on to something, Jennie. We were there for close to an hour trying to find Mancini's notes."

"Is that when you called me?"

"Yeah. I wanted you to be there."

"I'm glad I wasn't."

Gavin shot her a menacing look. "Just shut up and listen. Anyway, at around seven I told him I was leaving and stepped outside and closed the door. That's the last thing I remember until I woke up in some kind of meth lab—I know that's what it was because it had that strange smell."

"Where was Curtis while all this was going on?"

"He didn't hear a thing and thought I'd just gone home. He felt pretty awful. Told me it should have been him instead of me."

"Do you think whoever abducted you made a mistake?"

"Maybe." Gavin closed his eyes then opened them again. "I wondered about it, but I think they might have just wanted me out of the way. See, before Mancini's murder I'd been snooping around, asking questions. Maybe I just got too close. I just wish I could remember more. Like I told the police, they kept me drugged, and when they let me go they blindfolded me."

"You didn't see their faces?"

"No. I just know there were a lot of them. I heard vehicles coming and going all the time."

"Motorcycles?"

"Some, but there were cars and trucks too. I think I even heard a helicopter once." Jennie followed Gavin's gaze to the door.

"Excuse me." A woman in a white lab coat stepped into the room carrying a tray. "I'm afraid I'll have to ask you to step out for a moment, miss. I need to draw some blood."

Douglas followed her in. "Bad timing, I see."

"This will only take a minute." The woman whipped the curtains around Gavin's bed and disappeared behind them. Jennie followed Douglas out of the room.

"I hate to cut your visit short, but I need to leave. I'll have to come back and talk to him later. Would you mind if I dropped you off at your aunt's place now?"

"No, that's okay. Just let me say goodbye."

He nodded. "I'll meet you at the entrance in about five minutes."

Jennie waited until the nurse left, then went back in. "I have to go."

"I wish you could stay. Jennie, I really feel bad about this. I should have been straight with you from the start."

"Me too, but I understand why you did it. I just wish you hadn't planted the crank in my car. Evidence like that is hard to refute."

Gavin frowned. "What are you talking about? I didn't plant anything in your car."

"Gavin, how would you know? You were stoned out of your mind."

"I would have remembered that—I think. I remember crawling into your car. Thought I'd be safe there, but you went for help. I couldn't let the police see me like that. I was doing crazy stuff and . . . I guess I must have been acting pretty weird. Maybe you're right—maybe I did plant the stuff, but I don't remember. But if I did, I didn't do it on purpose."

"It's okay. Hopefully we'll be able to find out who's responsible for all this. I'm glad you finally decided to confide in me. Which reminds me, why did you?"

"When the police told me you'd been shot at, I realized it wouldn't make a difference whether I did what they said or not. I think they're planning to kill us both."

"I think you're right. I'll tell Agent Douglas and Lieutenant Rastovski what you said. Maybe they'll be able to solve the case before—well, before it's too late."

"Be careful," Gavin warned as Jennie turned to go.

On her way out, the impact of Gavin's words and the shooting of the night before took on an ominous reality. The fact that someone was out to kill her hadn't fully registered. "Oh, God," she prayed in the confines of the elevator. "I don't want to die. And I don't want Gavin to die either."

The elevator doors opened and Jennie stepped out, nearly colliding with a heavyset man wearing a black T-shirt and black jeans. Her face came within two inches of his scraggly gray beard. She gasped and stepped back inside.

"Sorry, ma'am." He smiled, revealing a couple of gold fillings. His long hair had been pulled back into a ponytail.

"It's okay." Jennie ducked out, trying not to stare at the hairy, tattooed arm that reached out to hold the door open. The man stepped into the elevator and nodded to her again as the doors slid shut. Jennie released the breath she'd been holding and chastised herself for being so jumpy. It hadn't helped that the tattoo had been a skull with two roses crossed beneath it. Strange.

She hurried to meet Douglas, all the while telling herself that she and Gavin would be fine. Dad and Douglas would make certain nothing happened to them.

Jennie hauled in a lungful of air and swallowed back her fears. With her shoulders straight and her head high, she exited the building and headed for Douglas's car. Her hand on the door handle, Jennie paused. The hair raised on the back of her neck and an odd chill ran through her veins like ice water. Was the shooter out there?

Glancing around behind her, she yanked the car door open and slipped inside. At least there she'd be safe.

Jennie slammed the door and scanned the hospital entry. "I could be wrong," she said, "but I think someone was following—"

Her thoughts froze as she turned toward the driver. Jennie stared at the cold, steel blue eyes, then dropped her gaze to the gun in the driver's hand.

# 21

Jennie pressed back against the door and groped for the handle. He was already moving, but maybe she could make a jump for it.

"Don't even think about it." He raised the gun for emphasis. "Just turn around and put your seat belt on. We're going to take a nice little ride."

Jennie did as she'd been told. She had to stay calm. *Look for a means of escape. But not yet. Play along. Wait for the right moment.* She just hoped that moment would come.

"That's a good girl. Now fold your hands and put them on your lap where I can see them." He chuckled and snapped a pair of handcuffs over her wrists.

"Who . . . who are you? Where's Douglas?"

The man sneered. "Let's just say he got a little testy about my wanting to borrow his car. Had to get a little forceful."

She glanced back. Douglas was lying on the seat, unconscious, blood caked on his nose and cheek. "Is he . . . dead?"

"Naw, not yet. Couldn't very well shoot him in the parking lot, could I? Besides, I got a much better means of getting rid of both of you."

Jennie willed her heart to slow down. At the rate it was pounding it would beat itself to death on her rib cage. "Who are you?" She forced herself to examine the driver closely. If she ever did make it out alive, she wanted to be able to identify her assailant. He looked vaguely familiar, but Jennie couldn't place him.

"You don't know me, Jennie McGrady, but I know you. My little brother seems to think you're worth saving, which is about the only thing that's kept me from blowing you away before now."

"You—you're the one who shot at me last night?" She could see the family resemblance now—Ray Bolton, Curtis's brother. Only he didn't look at all like the executive type—even though he was wearing an expensive-looking suit. Amazing how a gun could alter one's appearance.

The gun clunked against the steering wheel as he rolled down the window. Wind whipped loose strands of sun-bleached kinky hair into his face. "You've got it all wrong, Jennie. I'd never indulge in that kind of thing—especially not when there are so many guys out there who could use the work."

"You paid someone to kill me? Why?"

"You're a witness. You know too much. I'd have had someone blow you away sooner, but Curtis didn't think you'd be a problem." He set the gun on the seat beside him. "You got lucky last night, but I don't intend to let that happen again."

Jennie pretended not to notice, keeping her eyes focused on his face. Maybe he'd get distracted and she could grab the gun.

He pulled a pack of cigarettes out of his shirt pocket and tapped it against his hand, then pulled one free with his lips. "Want one?" He handed the pack over to her.

Jennie shrank back and shook her head. "I don't smoke."

"That's good. These things'll kill you." He chuckled and lit his cigarette, drew in deeply, and blew a thick stream of smoke in her face. "'Course, there are other things even more dangerous. Like sticking your nose in where it doesn't belong."

Jennie coughed. Using the driver's side controls, Ray lowered her window.

"Where are you taking me?"

Leaving the hospital parking lot, he turned right on Sunnyside Road and was heading out into the country—toward the Winslows' farm. Curtis lived out there as well. "You'll see soon enough." Smoke escaped in puffs as he spoke.

Jennie watched the houses whiz by. Soon the housing developments would give way to farmland. There was a corn field, Jennie remembered, on the right-hand side of the road, where you turn to go to Gavin's. If he turned there, maybe she could jump out of the car. Maybe she could use the field for cover. With any luck she might be able to outrun him.

Ray slowed down when he reached Delemeter Road and flipped on the indicator. Good, he was turning right. She glanced out at the field. Her spirits plummeted. The corn was there all right, about ten feet inside a high barbed wire fence. She'd never be able to vault the fence and make it to the corn in time. Jennie took some slow, deep breaths to settle herself down and prayed for another opportunity.

Ray picked up speed again and bounced along the potholed road. Jennie could see the Winslow place ahead. All kinds of scenarios drifted through Jennie's head as she frantically looked for escape routes. Both of the Winslows' cars were gone, which meant there'd be no one to help. Even if she managed to get to the house, she couldn't get in.

As if sensing her escape plans, Ray picked up the gun and trained it on her. "If you're thinking of running, I wouldn't."

*Okay*, Jennie bit her lip and tried to think rationally. *It won't do any good to panic. Douglas is still alive. He has to wake up soon.* And when he did, they could work together.

Jennie's fists tightened in determination. She'd always been a fighter and no way would she give up now. "Since you're planning to kill me anyway, why don't you tell me what's going on?"

"You're too much. Why don't you just shut up? You'll find out soon enough."

About half a mile past the Winslows', the road curved to the east, then south again and dead-ended at a huge new house that sat on a knoll. Ray passed the circular driveway, cut through a short stretch of field, then turned onto a narrow, windy dirt road. After a few minutes, he jammed on the brakes in front of a fence. "Stay put." Ray waved the gun at her, then jumped out.

In the few seconds it took for him to undo the latch and swing the gate inward, Jennie reached for the car radio. She pressed down on the button to send. With so many things to say, she wasn't sure where to begin. "This is an emergency. Agent Douglas has been injured. We're just south of Bo—"

The sentence ended in a scream as Ray reached in though the passenger-side window, grabbed a handful of hair, and yanked her back against the seat.

She raised her arms to ward off his fist.

Ray gritted his teeth and swore, then ran around to the driver's side. Reaching inside, he yanked the radio wires loose, cutting off the dispatcher in midsentence.

Jennie whimpered and closed her eyes. Her arm throbbed where he'd smashed his fist into it. She cowered against the door.

"Don't try anything like that again," he snapped. "You mess me up and I'll make sure that cute little brother of yours doesn't make it to his next birthday."

*No. Not Nick.* She sniffed, not daring to say anything in case she'd make him more angry.

"I see that got your attention." He drove through the opening but didn't bother to get out to fasten the gate again.

*Pull yourself together, McGrady.* Jennie tried giving herself another pep talk. It wasn't doing much good. She hadn't been able to give much information to the dispatch operator. Jennie prayed it would be enough. She'd always been taught to think positively. But there weren't many positives left. Even if the police figured out what she'd been trying to say, she doubted it would do any good. The Boltons' house was over a mile away. By the time the police found this place, if they ever found it, she and Douglas would be dead.

Ray pulled up in front of an older white two-story house. Half a dozen motorcycles and a large late model motor home cluttered the overgrown front yard. A couple of stripped-down rusty car skeletons sat half buried in the tall dry grass beside the house. A bed of pink and white impatiens grew in the shade beside some rickety wooden steps.

Two men wearing leathers and chains stepped onto the small, cluttered porch carrying the biggest flask Jennie had ever seen.

It didn't take a genius to figure out what they'd been doing. This must have been the meth lab Gavin had mentioned.

"'Bout time you got here, Ray," the man facing them said. "Beginnin' to think ya'd run out on us."

"Not likely. Just had some last-minute details to take care of." He glared at Jennie, then turned back to the men. "You guys almost done here? We don't have much time."

"Got most of it. Couple more trips."

"Good. Remember to leave enough supplies in the kitchen to make it look like a small operation."

"Right. We left most of what we took from that school your brother goes to." They carried the flask to the motor home and set it inside, then headed back to the house.

From what she'd learned about clandestine labs from Rocky, this was a typical setup. Take over a vacant house, set up a lab for a few weeks, then move on. These guys looked like they'd done this sort of thing before.

Looked like Douglas and Rastovski—Dad—had been wrong about one thing. Curtis and Mancini hadn't been using Trinity's lab. A wave of grief crashed through her when she thought of Dad. All these years of wishing and praying and hoping he'd come home, and now that he finally had she wasn't going to be around long enough to enjoy it.

Jennie shook off the dismal thought. She wondered what Dad would do in her place—or Gram or J.B. *They wouldn't give up*, a voice inside her seemed to say. *And neither will you.*

"Looks like you're getting ready to leave." Jennie's voice came out surprisingly strong.

"How very astute."

"Ray." Curtis appeared in the doorway. "What took you so—" His startled gaze swept to Jennie. "What's she doing here? I told you—"

"Let's get something straight, little brother." Ray grabbed hold of Jennie's arm and dragged her toward the steps. "From now on, you don't tell me anything. I'm running things around here, and don't you forget it."

"But—"

"Forget her. And the Winslow kid. If you want to work for me, you can't afford to get personally involved."

The look on Curtis's face told Jennie he didn't want to work for Ray. Only Ray was the type of person who didn't take no for an answer.

"Did you get that last batch set up?"

Curtis nodded. "I still don't understand why you're leaving all this stuff. Between the equipment and the latest batch of crank, you're looking at close to thirty grand."

"More like forty, but like I told you before, that's part of the expense of doing business. Keeps the cops off our tails. We go in, set up shop, make a few bucks, then close things down. After we're gone the cops get an anonymous tip, come out, and find a two-bit operation run by local high school kids."

"You're not going to get away with this," Jennie said. "Do

you honestly think the police will believe I'm running a meth lab?"

"Why not? They arrested you for possession. The way I see it, you and the Winslow kid had a profitable business going here. Unfortunately, you got scared. You went to see your friend, Winslow, and slipped him a lethal dose of heroin."

Jennie jerked away. "You killed Gavin? What kind of an animal are you?"

He laughed, adding fuel to the rage welling up inside her.

"You are not going to get away with this."

"Watch me." Ray raised his pistol. "I had planned on letting you take an overdose of the drug you've been cooking up, but I can just as well shoot you. See, Agent Douglas was on to you. He followed you out here, and when you tried to escape he shot you. Then he goes into the house to investigate and trips our little booby trap. Poor guy can't make it out of the house in time."

"You tell a great story, Ray, but the police aren't going to buy it."

"Jennie, shut up. You're just making things worse." Curtis jumped down from the steps and stepped between his brother and Jennie. "Ray, please. Leave her alone."

"Get out of my way." Ray pushed Curtis aside, but Curtis outweighed Ray by about thirty pounds.

"No, you'll have to shoot me first."

"The boy's right, Ray." Douglas walked toward them. "Shooting Jennie would be a big mistake. But not as big as jumping me and stealing my car." He stretched his hand toward Ray. "Give me my gun."

Ray shook his head. "You're a bigger fool that I thought."

Douglas dove at Ray, knocking him to the ground. The gun went off. Jennie dropped to her knees and crawled to the steps. Hunkering down beside them, she tried to stay out of the line of fire as the two men fought for possession of the gun.

Curtis crouched down behind her. "I'm so sorry you had to get involved in this, Jennie. I never meant—"

The gun went off again. The two men lay in a motionless heap in the bed of flowers. Douglas lay on the bottom. A crimson stain began to spread across Ray Bolton's back. Douglas pushed the injured Ray aside and got to his feet.

Curtis yelped like a wounded dog and ran to his brother's side.

Jennie shuddered and looked away, relieved yet horrified. Now what? Douglas had taken out one man, but there were others. As if to prove her point, five men all looking like members of a notorious motorcycle gang moved out from behind vehicles and stepped outside the motor home and house where they'd apparently taken cover. They stood their ground, as if daring Douglas to make a move. All of them, Jennie noticed, wore the same tattoo on their forearms as the man she'd seen at the hospital—the one who had probably been sent to kill Gavin.

Not knowing what to do or what to expect, Jennie pressed herself against the foundation, wishing she could disappear into the rotting wood.

"Put him in the backseat of my car and get Curtis into the house." Douglas barked the order, and to Jennie's surprise two of the men looked as if they were going to obey him.

As he holstered his gun, terror streaked through her like a lightning bolt. DEA Agent Steve Douglas was one of them.

# 22

"Get in the house." Douglas walked toward her. His rumpled suit and bloodstained shirt made him look like a villain in a monster movie. Dried blood still clung to his face where Ray had hit him. For a brief moment Jennie wondered if maybe the bikers were with the DEA, but only for a moment.

Jennie straightened and started up the steps, then turned back to face him. "Why?"

His eyebrow arched. "Money. What else? Do you have any idea what it's like to watch these thugs get wealthier by the day? I worked my tail off trying to fight the President's war on drugs, and what do I have to show for it?—squat. I can pull in more in in a day manufacturing drugs than I can in a year working for the government."

"You betrayed the other agents—my father. Dad trusted you. You were the informer that nearly got him killed, weren't you?" Douglas had probably been leaking information to the drug dealers all along. No wonder Dad's enemies could so easily track him down. It had been too dangerous for him to come home—now she knew why.

"It's war, Jennie." She thought she might have seen a flicker of regret pass through his eyes, but if she did, it quickly disappeared. "Now move."

She took another step and stopped again. "W-what are you going to do with me?"

"Not a thing. You see, that's the beauty of it. My hands are clean."

*No, they aren't,* Jennie wanted to say. *They're covered with blood. Not just Ray's, but the DEA agents' who trusted you.*

Douglas nodded toward his car. "In a little over an hour, I'll be heading back into town with Ray Bolton's body. I'll be credited with breaking up yet another drug operation. And with finding Dr. Mancini's killer.

"Thing is, I'll have some bad news. You see, Jennie, in raiding this meth lab, my good friend, Lieutenant Rastovski, gets caught in a deadly booby trap set, of course, by Ray Bolton and his little band of honor students. He goes into the house to rescue you and Curtis while I go after Ray, but by the time I manage to take Ray down everyone in the house is dead. It'll make a great story, don't you think?"

The bitterness in his tone dripped like acid on Jennie's heart, eating away at any hope she had left of getting out alive. "Why? You don't have to bring my father into it."

"Save the tears, kid. Sooner or later he'd figure out who's behind the leaks. He's already asking questions. I can't take that chance. Now get inside."

"No one will believe you. The police will find us tied up— they'll know we're innocent."

"You won't be tied up when they find you. And as for believing me." He shook his head. "Jennie, Jennie. I'm a DEA agent. You and the Winslow kid have been caught with drugs—"

"You planted the crank in my car?"

He didn't need to answer. Jennie could see the admission written all over his face.

"Joey," he yelled over his shoulder at one of the bikers. "Tell Buck to get the motor home ready. We'd better move now if we want to hit Spokane by nightfall. We'll go ahead with the plan we had before—just a few alterations."

"You got it." A big burly guy with a scraggly beard and

black eyes signaled one of the other bikers.

"I said get inside." Douglas gave her a push. Jennie tripped on the threshold and went sprawling across the entry. He pulled her up and released one end of the handcuffs still circling Jennie's wrist, then hauled her to the staircase. "Sit down."

Jennie sniffed and dragged her hand across her eyes. The room reaked like a litter box that hadn't been cleaned in months. *This is it, McGrady. You're going to die.* The whole world would think she was a drug dealer. Except Mom and Gram.

Douglas wrapped the chain around the newel post at the bottom of the stairs, then snapped the cuff back on her wrist. "That ought to hold you." He went outside and came back a few minutes later wearing a clean suit. He'd washed the blood off his hands and face. Clean. How ironic that people who looked cleanest on the outside were often the blackest on the inside.

Jennie heard the motor home start up and drive away. A few minutes later Joey came in with Curtis. "What do you want me to do with the kid?"

"Tie him to the stairs beside Jennie. They can comfort each other."

Joey did as he'd been told, then joined Douglas in the kitchen. "So, what's the plan?"

Jennie could no longer see them. Unfortunately, she could hear them all too well. She inched closer to the railing, away from Curtis, and rested her head against the post.

"The cops are going to find two kids in here instead of one. With Ray dead, there's no reason to take Curtis with us. I don't trust him to keep his mouth shut. Unfortunately, the kid's got a conscience."

"He's one of the best cooks we've ever had."

"We'll find another one. Every town has its share of chemists."

"What about the formula? The only reason Ray wanted the kid along was because of the pill Dr. Mancini developed. We can't afford to let a drug like that hit the market."

Jennie's head jerked up. She glanced at Curtis. So Mancini really had been working on an anti-addiction pill. The conspiracy theory hadn't been all that far-fetched after all. Who more than these drug manufacturers would want to prevent a medication like that from being available to the public?

"We don't have to worry about that," Douglas added. "Mrs. Mancini was all too happy to hand her husband's computer disks over to me. Wanted to make sure her husband's lifelong work didn't get into the wrong hands. Right now they're in the evidence locker down at the station."

"But—"

Douglas chuckled. "I phonied them up. Erased his research data and replaced it with a couple recipes for designer drugs. My report will reflect the latter. Sad, isn't it? You can't trust anybody these days. Seems as though Dawson Pharmaceuticals payed Mancini for research he never did."

Joey chuckled. "I gotta hand it to you, boss. You don't miss a trick."

Douglas came out of the kitchen carrying a tin pie plate, which he set on the floor near the door. Joey followed with another dish and a coil of twine.

"Ever see an acid trap, Jennie?" Douglas took the container from Joey and held it up. "It's really very simple—but effective. We rig this up so the unlucky stiff who opens the door inadvertently pulls the acid container over. The acid spills into the sodium cyanide crystals." He pointed to the pie tin on the floor. "When mixed, these two ingredients create a deadly gas. "This one's especially potent. One whiff can kill you."

"You're not going to get away with this," Jennie said

again. Maybe if she said it often enough and believed hard enough it would be true.

"Of course I am, Jennie. I'm one of the best DEA agents in the business. Your dad will vouch for that."

"He won't come out here alone. He'll bring half a dozen units with him."

Douglas nodded. "That's what I'm counting on. I'll call in my location and meet them at the end of the road. We'll head out in different directions looking for Ray Bolton. See, after Bolton jumped me and abducted you, I managed to escape. I'm not sure where he went—only that it's down in this general area. We'll split up in pairs. My long-time partner and I will come back here. Like I said before, he'll be intent on rescuing you. Now, Jennie, if you'll excuse me, I need to get these guys on the road and make a phone call."

"I'll scream. I'll warn him and he won't come in."

"Sorry, Jennie. If you do that, I'll be forced to shoot him in the back. Or rather Ray will shoot him—and I'll be forced to kill Ray. Any way you play it, I can't lose."

Douglas turned to the biker. "Joey, there's some duct tape on the counter in the kitchen. You know what to do with it. Be sure to secure the doors when you leave."

Joey ripped off a strip of gray tape and pressed it over Jennie's mouth and repeated the procedure with Curtis. He tossed the tape aside and, after setting the booby trap, stepped outside.

A few minutes later Jennie heard the rev of engines as the motorcycles departed in tandem. They were all gone now, except for Douglas. He was out on the porch calling his old friend Jason McGrady, alias Nate Rastovski, for backup.

Jennie ducked her face to her hands and peeled off the tape. Joey wasn't too bright. He should have put their hands behind their backs, not left them in front. Not that being able to talk did much good. If she tried to warn Dad, Douglas would shoot him. Jennie had to find a way to disarm the booby trap or at least get out of there before Douglas and her father came back. Things looked pretty bleak, but Jennie held tight to God's promise that all things are possible to those who believe. There had to be a way out.

She wrapped her hands around the four-inch-thick carved post Douglas had handcuffed her to, trying to pull it free or break it.

"It's no use, Jennie," Curtis murmured after he'd removed the tape from his mouth. "The only thing that will bust these posts is an axe."

Jennie glared at him. "Don't talk to me, you creep."

"I—" Curtis heaved a shuddering sigh. "I'm sorry. I didn't want to have anything to do with this. They forced me to cook for them. They stole equipment from the lab at school and threatened to blame it on me. Later they threatened to kill Gavin—and you. I should have told the police the truth when I had a chance, but I couldn't. Ray's my brother."

Jennie shook her head. "And that's supposed to make things okay?"

"No, it's just . . ."

"You know what really burns me? You come over to my house with this 'You gotta help me find Mr. Mancini's killer' garbage, and all the while you were one of them. Which reminds me, why did you tell the police and me about Dr. Mancini's anti-addiction drug?"

"Ray told me to. Said it would take the heat off us. Look, Jennie, I didn't want to get involved in this—you gotta believe that. Besides, what I said was true. Ray wanted me to destroy Dr. Mancini's formula. Said some guy offered to pay him five hundred grand to make sure the anti-addiction pills never hit the market."

"Douglas?"

Curtis nodded. "I didn't know Douglas was involved until last night when Ray told me it was time to get rid of his boss and strike out on his own." He chewed on his lower lip. "I guess his plans kind of backfired."

"Is that what you were trying to do the day Mancini was killed? What happened, did he interrupt your plans?"

Curtis glanced over at her. "Yeah. Ray forced me to go with him to the school that afternoon. I didn't know Dr. Mancini would be there—or you. He was working in the lab and must have heard us talking in his office. He threatened to call the police. Ray pulled a gun on him and he ran back into the lab. I went after him and tried to talk to him, but . . ."

The pained expression in his eyes told Jennie more than she wanted to know. "You killed him?"

"I didn't mean to. He came at me and I pushed him back. He fell against the counter in the lab and hit his head. I couldn't believe he was dead. I wanted to call the police, but Ray—Ray put the gun in Dr. Mancini's hand."

" . . . and set things up to look like a suicide," Jennie finished.

Curtis nodded. "Things went downhill from there. You showed up, and I thought he was going to kill you. We hid behind the counter. I kept praying you wouldn't see us or Mancini. I knew if you had, Ray would have killed you too."

Tears stung her eyes. "The noise I heard came from the office."

"We'd left the door ajar—the wind must have opened it more and blown some of Mancini's notes off the desk."

"And when I left, you took them."

"They were notes and correspondence pertaining to the anti-addiction drug. When you left, I grabbed the papers and erased the formula from the disk. Ray made me type a suicide note."

"But you used Alex instead of Alexis. You, of all people, must have known how Dr. Mancini felt about his step-daughter's name."

"I did. I guess I wanted the police to know it wasn't a

suicide. I told Ray I didn't want any more to do with him and his thugs. That's when he threatened to kill you and Gavin if I didn't cooperate."

In the distance Jennie could hear the wail of sirens. She sucked in a long, slow breath to stem the panic rising inside her, then wished she hadn't. The putrid smell of the meth-amphetamine still cooking in the kitchen gagged her. She wretched, then coughed.

"Breathe through your mouth and it's not so bad."

Jennie nodded. "Douglas will be back with Lieutenant Rastovski any minute. You got any ideas?"

"Maybe, if I can just reach the sodium cyanide with my foot and kick it away. When the door opens the acid would still tip over, but at least it won't be toxic. It's our only chance."

"Try it. Just be careful." The way the mechanism worked, if Curtis accidentally snagged his foot on the chair holding the acid, it would be over for both of them. "Better take off your shoes or you'll never get your foot under the chair."

Curtis removed his shoes, then stretched out on the floor and eased his foot under the chair. His toe was still at least six inches from the pie tin—it may as well have been a mile. "It's no use."

"Let me try it." Jennie wasn't quite as tall, but she had been handcuffed to the side closest to the trap. She slipped off her sneakers, rolled over on her side, and extended one leg.

"Look out, the chair."

Jennie pulled her foot back. Holding her breath, Jennie eased her foot under the rung of the scarred wooden chair. She pressed the top of her foot against the pie tin and inched it forward. "I'm getting it." When her foot touched the front chair leg, she stopped.

"It's not far enough," she breathed. "When the acid comes down it's still going to hit the bowl."

"Okay. What you're going to have to do is kick it as hard as you can across the floor. With any luck the tin will slide on the linoleum."

"But I'll hit the chair."

"I know, and the acid will go flying, but if you can shove the plate far enough away and if the acid doesn't spill. . . . Just make sure you pull your foot back fast."

Jennie didn't have to ask why. If the acid landed on her foot, she'd probably lose it. Jennie closed her eyes and said a prayer. She went through the motions in her mind, planning each detail. *Do it, McGrady*, she coached herself. *Do it now*.

She heard muffled voices outside. Douglas was back. Any minute now, Dad would be coming through the front door. Jennie laid her foot alongside the tin.

Footsteps sounded on the steps outside. *Please don't spill. Please . . . please . . . please.* Jennie swallowed hard. And kicked. She jerked back and screamed as the acid crashed to the floor.

# 23

"You did it." Curtis leaned toward her. "The acid—did you?"

"No. I don't think I got any on me." Jennie grabbed the post at the base of the stairs and pulled herself back onto the step.

The front door flew open and slammed against the wall.

Lieutenant Rastovski stared at the mess barring his way. "What the—" His gaze traveled across the entry and landed on Jennie. He shoved the chair aside and stepped across the pool of acid now eating through the cheap linoleum. "Thank God you're all right."

"Douglas is behind all this. He's going to kill you."

"What are you talking about?"

The porch steps creaked and a shadow filled the doorway. "You must live a charmed life, McGrady. Or you have until now." Douglas raised his revolver and clicked back the hammer. He fired. Jennie screamed.

The force of the bullet knocked Rastovski back. He leapt forward and slammed into the man who had called himself a friend. Douglas grunted and flew backward, landing on the porch steps. Rastovski dove on top of him.

Though only seconds passed, it seemed like forever before her father moved away from Douglas's still form. The detective clutched at his chest and staggered back inside.

Again careful to overt the acid, he dropped down on the stairs beside Jennie, a key to the handcuffs in his hand. He managed to release her before collapsing on the entry floor.

"Dad—" Had he been shot? Jennie couldn't see an injury and felt a moment of relief when she saw he was wearing a bulletproof vest.

He moaned and grimaced. "Think I broke a rib—" His breaths were shallow and ragged, and Jennie suspected the injury was much more serious than that. Possibly a punctured lung.

"Don't try to talk. I'll go for help."

"Wait," he gasped. "Take my gun. Signal for help. Three shots."

"Three shots. Got it."

Once outside again, she aimed upward, gripped the handle of the gun, and fired. The recoil nearly knocked her to the ground. She steadied herself and fired two more shots, set the gun on the planter, then took off running. With any luck she'd find Dad's car phone to call an ambulance. As she rounded the first bend Jennie spotted a squad car. She waved for the officer to stop. Officer Phelps paused long enough to hear Jennie's explanation, then called for backup. "Get in." She was on the move before Jennie could get the door closed.

"You'd better have someone check on Gavin Winslow." Jennie braced herself against the dash for the rough ride back to the farmhouse.

Phelps tossed her a questioning look.

"I'll explain later. I just hope we're not too late."

She picked up the radio and asked the dispatch operator to send someone over to Sunnyside, then scrambled out of the car. A second squad car, then a third, pulled into the driveway behind them.

———

After riding to the hospital in the ambulance with her father, Jennie spent most of the next two hours answering questions and explaining what had happened and who had done what. She told the police everything except the fact that Nate Rastovski was actually her father. She couldn't remember if Curtis had heard her call him dad. Not that it mattered. At the moment, Curtis was too busy confessing his involvement in Mancini's murder and the drug operation and giving the police a rundown on one of the most sophisticated drug rings in the country. The state patrol would soon be picking up the bikers and the motor home heading for Spokane.

"I think that's about it, Jennie." Officer Phelps tucked her notebook into her back pocket. "We'll probably have more questions later. I . . . um—what you did in disarming that booby trap—you saved Lieutenant Rastovski's life. I can see now why Officer Rockwell thinks so highly of you. You managed to stay cool under extreme circumstances. You're going to make a good cop someday."

"Thanks. Uh—have you heard anything about Gavin?"

"Sure did. You were right. Ray had one of his crew visit Gavin right after you left. A nurse walked in and caught him getting ready to inject your friend with a hefty dose of heroin. When she tried to stop him, he took off. A couple of security guards caught up with him and called the police before he could leave the hospital. Your friend lucked out. If that nurse hadn't come along when she did, he'd never have made it."

"More than luck. I prayed a lot."

Devon nodded and pressed her lips together. "I'd better get back to the station—this is going to be one heck of a report to fill out. Can I drop you off or anything?"

"No, I want to be here when Lieutenant Rastovski gets out of surgery."

---

Jennie paced the waiting room floor in the surgical unit. Dad had broken a rib all right and punctured a lung. They were putting in a chest tube to suck the air out of the chest cavity so his lung could reinflate. The surgeon had assured her he'd be fine in a few days.

Twice Jennie started to call Mom to let her know. But what could she say? *"Mom. Your new boyfriend's been hurt. But he's not really Nate Rastovski, Mom, he's your husband. And guess what, Mom, I was abducted and almost died."* Not something you could tell your mom over the phone.

She stopped at the pay phone, inserted a quarter, and dialed home again, this time waiting for Mom to answer.

"Hello?"

Her grandmother's warm greeting sent a flurry of relief through Jennie. "Oh, Gram, I'm so glad you're there. I have to talk to you. Dad's in surgery and Mom still doesn't know he's back."

"Whoa . . . slow down, darling—what are you talking about?"

Jennie blurted out the morning's disastrous events, her visit to Gavin, the abduction, the DEA agent and his double life as a drug lord, and the fact that Lieutenant Nate Rastovski was actually her father.

"Jennie, you're certain of that? Only this morning we learned that Jason had left the DEA and would be surfacing under a different name, but we didn't expect it would be so soon."

"I don't think he meant it to be, but with me being involved in the Mancini murder case, it just happened. We have to tell Mom."

"She isn't here, Jennie. I'm not sure where she's gone." Gram paused. "We—J.B. and I thought it might be best if she knew Jason was still alive before he actually contacted her. We felt she should be prepared. Now I'm not certain that was such a good idea."

"What did she say?"

"Not much, I'm afraid. She's very upset."

After promising to get to the hospital right away, Gram hung up.

Jennie paced. How could one family get so messed up? And talk about confusion. Now Mom knew Dad was alive, but she didn't know Dad was Nate Rastovski. Jennie shuddered to think of how Mom would react when she found that out. Dad should have told her right away. What frightened Jennie most though was the uncertainty surrounding her father. Would he stay in Portland like he'd said? Douglas was no longer a threat, but how many others like him were out there? Jennie didn't want to think about that. She had to get hold of Mom.

Leaning against the wall next to the phone, Jennie tried to imagine where Mom would go.

*Michael. Maybe she went to see Michael.*

Jennie called the church. Michael wasn't in. He'd gone to lunch with Mom. "Would you like to leave a message?" Sarah asked.

"Yes. Tell my mom that Lieutenant Rastovski's been shot."

"Oh, my goodness. Isn't he the man working on Mr. Mancini's murder?"

"Yeah. Um—he's in surgery right now." Jennie told her where.

"I'll be sure to tell her. Would you like me to put Mr. Rastovski on our prayer chain?"

"I think that would be a good idea. Thanks."

Prayer—she could use some herself. Nothing short of divine intervention could help them now. Jennie made her way to the small chapel on the first floor. She slipped into the backseat and bowed her head. Light streamed through the stained-glass window of Jesus holding the lost sheep. *God, I just wanted to thank you for bringing Dad home. Now I need another favor. Please, please let him be okay.* Bathed in rainbows from the sun streaming through the colored glass, Jennie felt almost as though she'd been visited by an angel. Smiling, she remembered a television program about angels visiting the earth and helping people through difficult times.

"I wish you'd send me an angel, God," Jennie murmured. "And one to Mom. Make her see that Dad loves her and needs her. Tell her to break up with Michael." The lights blurred as tears gathered in her eyes and dripped down her cheeks.

"God doesn't work that way, darling." Gram slipped into the pew next to Jennie. "You know that. He won't *make* your mother break her engagement to Michael or remarry your father. She has to make those decisions on her own."

Jennie took the tissue Gram handed her and dabbed at her eyes. "But God is supposed to answer our prayers."

"God does answer prayer—but sometimes His answers aren't always what we'd like them to be."

Jennie sighed. "I want us all back together as a family. But I want Mom and Dad to be happy—not like they were before."

"Do you think that's possible?"

"Anything is possible, but it's not likely, is it?"

Gram gave her a hug and suggested they go see how her father was doing. They walked arm in arm back to the surgical unit. Jennie's heart felt heavier than a truckload of rocks. She tried to lighten the load by concentrating on the positives. Dr. Mancini's murderer and a ruthless drug ring had been captured. Gavin was safe. She, Dad, and Curtis had survived what might have been a deathtrap. All in all, a good day. And there was still a chance Mom would be happy when she learned that Nate Rastovski was really her husband—ex-husband. Still a chance that she'd dump Michael, remarry Dad, and live happily ever after. Okay, a *remote* possibility.

# 24

"Come on, Jennie, everyone's waiting." Lisa pulled at her cousin's arm.

Jennie stood in front of the mirror in Lisa's bedroom wishing the world would suddenly come to an end. Weddings were supposed to be joyous affairs, but Jennie felt anything but. "You go ahead. I'll be down in a minute."

"All right, but hurry. They're going to start the processional in five minutes." Lisa turned to go, her pink satin bridesmaid's dress swirled around her ankles, showing off the matching satin pumps.

She looked gorgeous—they all did. Even Jennie felt pretty. Her hair piled on her head, then cascading down in dozens of ringlets. Jennie's dress, a duplicate of Lisa's, showed off her slender figure.

She padded to the window and stared down into Kate's and Kevin's backyard. Thirty white wooden folding chairs had been set in five rows of six, separated down the middle by a four-foot band of lawn. The bridal party would walk out of the house, across the deck, and through an arched trellis. Decorated in ribbons and all types of colorful flowers, it looked like the perfect place for a romantic wedding. With only two days' notice, Aunt Kate had done a fantastic job. Only a few of the chairs toward the back were empty.

"I'm sorry, Dad," Jennie whispered. "I tried so hard to

talk her into marrying you instead of Michael. But you know Mom. Once she makes up her mind there isn't much anyone can say. I just wish you hadn't gone away again. That might have helped. Mom says you're unreliable. Maybe she has a point."

After spending three days in the hospital, Dad had gone to stay with Gram and J.B. at the coast. He'd only been there a couple of days when he went back to work. There were a lot of details to clear up, he'd said. Mom hadn't believed him—or hadn't wanted to. Now Jennie was beginning to wonder if he'd come back at all, or if he'd changed his name again and reenlisted in the war against drugs.

Mom still hadn't forgiven him for lying to her. She'd refused his phone calls and his flowers and told him she never wanted to see him again. Then in a move so totally unlike Mom, she decided to marry Michael—immediately. Jennie wondered what would have happened if Dad had stayed in Portland—or even stayed with Gram. Now she'd never know.

"There is one good thing in all of this," Jennie murmured. "Michael will make a great dad for Nick."

She hauled in a deep breath and squared her shoulders, then hurried downstairs to the family room to join the others. Kate, Mom's matron of honor, gathered everyone together. Clucking like a mother hen, she set them in their respective places for walking down the aisle. Kate hadn't said much when she'd learned that her twin brother was still alive. Maybe it hadn't sunk in yet. Or maybe she was angry with him too.

Either way, she'd supported Mom's decision to marry Michael. So had Gram, for that matter. Jennie couldn't understand how they could all be so gracious.

Kate had hired a guitarist from church to provide the music, and when she gave him the signal he started playing "The Wedding Song." The haunting refrain drifted through the yard, filling Jennie's heart with a bittersweet pain.

Michael, Pastor Dave, Uncle Kevin, and Kurt stood near a white wooden podium framed in large arrangements of pink and white gladiolus.

Nick started the procession. He looked adorable in his little tuxedo, carrying a pair of gold rings on a heart-shaped satin pillow. Bernie followed close at his heels, looking almost as important as his master.

Lisa stepped outside next, ducked through the trellis, and walked gracefully up to the front. Jennie was next. Just before stepping outside, she turned back to where Mom stood waiting. Their gazes met.

*Don't make trouble*, Mom's green eyes warned. She adjusted the lace-trimmed ivory gown.

Jennie's sent back a final plea. *Please, Mom, don't do this. You know you still love Dad.*

Mom broke eye contact, but not before Jennie saw a glimmer of uncertainty.

"Jennie, go." Kate gave her a little push and Jennie moved ahead, ducking through the vine-covered trellis. Step right—slide. Step left—slide. She kept her eyes focused on the podium. Reaching the front, she turned left, then stopped next to Lisa. Once Kate had taken her place, the music stopped. Everyone stood and waited for Mom to appear.

There wouldn't be a wedding march—Mom hadn't wanted that. She'd chosen a love song.

The guitarist strummed. Mom didn't come. After a few minutes, Gram, who'd been sitting with J.B. in the front row, excused herself and went back into the house.

Another five minutes went by. Jennie was getting worried. "I'm going in to see what's going on."

"Michael," Gram called from the patio. "I think you'd better come inside. You too, Pastor."

"Something's wrong with Mom." Jennie hurried inside as Kate began making excuses to the guests.

Mom was sitting on the floor in the middle of the dining

room, a ragged tissue balled up in her hand.

"Susan," Michael's voice was strained. "What happened?"

"Oh, Michael, I'm so sorry," Mom sobbed. "I thought I could go through with it. I wanted so much to love you, but I—"

Michael hunkered down beside her. "I don't understand. You seemed so sure."

"I know. I didn't want to hurt you. I thought if I could just make up my mind everything would be all right."

"You need more time. Is that it?" Michael cupped her elbow in his hand. "Listen—it's okay. We'll postpone the wedding for a few weeks or even a year."

Mom shook her head. "No, I can't. I've been lying to myself and you. The truth is, I'm still in love with Jason."

Michael straightened, his gray eyes misting like a storm on the ocean. His gaze traveled from Jennie to Gram, then settled on Pastor Dave. "I guess that's it, then. Maybe you could tell Kate and the others. . . . I'll be at the church."

One by one the guests offered their embarrassed goodbyes and left. Kate and Gram were doing their best to cheer Mom up. Lisa had gone up to her room to change. Jennie had changed earlier and was seriously thinking of going home.

"Hey!" Nick burst into the room and came to an abrupt halt in front of his mother. "Mama, why are you crying? Did you hurt yourself?"

"In a way, I guess I did."

He pulled at her hand. "Well, get over it. You have to come and see who I found. My dad's here."

"Don't be silly, Nick. Your father is . . ." She frowned at Jennie. "Did you tell him?"

"No, of course not." No one had told Nick about Dad— they'd all agreed it would be too traumatic and confusing for him—especially since Mom had decided to marry Michael.

"Slow down, Nick." Jennie snagged him as he flew past her. "What's going on?"

"It's my dad. He's here."

"Where?"

"Outside. He just got out of his car and is coming up the walk. Now Mom doesn't hafta marry Michael. We can have our real dad."

Mom blew her nose. "Jennie McGrady, if you've been filling this child's head with nonsense again, I'll—"

The front doorbell rang, and Jennie didn't wait for Mom to finish her accusation. She ran through the formal living room, into the entry, and yanked open the door.

"Dad—it *is* you." The dark brown contacts and mustache were gone. So were the silver streaks in his hair. Except for the scar, he looked like his picture.

"See, I told you." Nick scooted around her and took Dad's hand. "We been waiting a long time for you."

Jason McGrady grinned, scooped Nick into his arms, and stepped inside.

Once in the family room, Nick squirmed out of his dad's arms and ran down the hallway. "You stay here. I gotta go find Kurt. Boy, will he be surprised."

"Jason!" Gram opened her arms when he approached. "I'm so glad you decided to come back. I was beginning to wonder."

"I told you I would." He hugged Gram, then Kate. "What's going on here? Looks like a wedding." He frowned and let his cobalt gaze settle on Mom. "Susan, you didn't—"

"No, thanks to you, Nate Rastovski, or whoever you are these days."

He flinched. "I think you'll all be happy to know that I've decided to drop the charades. From now on I'm back to being Jason McGrady. Only I no longer work for the DEA. I did, however, decide to keep the job in Portland as an inspector in the homicide division."

"Really?" Mom eyed him warily.

"Won't that be dangerous?" Jennie asked. "What about the guys who were after you?"

"With Douglas out of the picture, we should be okay. I plan to keep a low profile—just hanging out with my family. It's going to take some getting used to, but if Susan's willing to give me another chance—" His gaze swept to Mom. "I know you said you didn't want to see me again, but I couldn't give up that easily. When we met for coffee that day, I suspected you still felt something for me. And I have never stopped loving you."

"Oh, Jason." Mom shook her head. "I don't know what to say."

Dad dropped down on his knees in front of her. "Don't say anything right now. Just think about it. In the meantime, how about having dinner with me?"

Mom nodded, then smiled. "All right, but we'd better take the kids. I think it's time they spent a little time with their father."

The heavy weight Jennie had been carrying around for a week finally fell away from her heart. It looked like her parents' love story might have a happy ending after all.

# Teen Series From
# Bethany House Publishers

## Early Teen Fiction (11–14)

HIGH HURDLES by Lauraine Snelling
Show jumper DJ Randall strives to defy the odds and achieve her dream of winning Olympic Gold.

SUMMERHILL SECRETS by Beverly Lewis
Fun-loving Merry Hanson encounters mystery and excitement in Pennsylvania's Amish country.

THE TIME NAVIGATORS by Gilbert Morris
Travel back in time with Danny and Dixie as they explore unforgettable moments in history.

## Young Adult Fiction (12 and up)

CEDAR RIVER DAYDREAMS by Judy Baer
Experience the challenges and excitement of high school life with Lexi Leighton and her friends—over one million books sold!

GOLDEN FILLY SERIES by Lauraine Snelling
Readers are in for an exhilarating ride as Tricia Evanston races to become the first female jockey to win the sought-after Triple Crown.

JENNIE MCGRADY MYSTERIES by Patricia Rushford
A contemporary Nancy Drew, Jennie McGrady's sleuthing talents promise to keep readers on the edge of their seats.

LIVE! FROM BRENTWOOD HIGH by Judy Baer
When eight teenagers invade the newsroom, the result is an action-packed teen-run news show exploring the love, laughter, and tears of high school life.

THE SPECTRUM CHRONICLES by Thomas Locke
Adventure and romance await readers in this fantasy series set in another place and time.

SPRINGSONG BOOKS by various authors
Compelling love stories and contemporary themes promise to capture the hearts of readers.

WHITE DOVE ROMANCES by Yvonne Lehman
Romance, suspense, and fast-paced action for teens committed to finding pure love.